The Advent
Bo

To be Human
or to be All

The Adventures of Julia Wang
Book One

To be Human
or to be All

by Eriqa Queen

Series title: The Adventures of Julia Wang
Title: To be Human or to be All
Number in series: 1
Copyright © Eriqa Queen 2022
Copyright © Erik Istrup Publishing 2022
Cover art by Erik Istrup Copyright © 2022
Published through IngramSpark
Font: Palatino
ISBN: 978-87-94110-26-6

Genre: Fantasy

This is the first title in the series

Erik Istrup Publishing
Jyllandsgade 16 stth, 9610 Nørager, Danmark
www.erikistrup.dk/publishing/ • eip@erikistrup.dk

Contents

Jumping on a running train

I am not used to beginnings, because time is not part of what I am. All is in the ocean of me, but there is no time nor space in my ocean. Jumping on a train at full speed would be a metaphor for beginning, and so make it a beginning. Here is a one anyway.

Hello, I am the consciousness or what you would call the soul of Julia Wang. I will change the definition of the term soul shortly in your linear time. I use present tense throughout the story, even if 'present' really makes little sense to me, and nor does 'now'. This might confuse my writing, but I will do my best to use a terminology the mind can understand. Not to say that I won't challenge your mind.

I am beginning the story before I was born into this life, explaining about what happened before my incarnation, my physical birth.

As I prepare the incarnation as Julia Wang, I consult the souls whom I have selected as my parents to find out how they feel about the arrangement. There will also be other souls involved.

When consciousness communicates, it happens outside time and space. This means that even a long conversation happens in an instant. Our conversations are over before they even begin, but still contain the fulness of them, as if they actually had been human conversations. Well, with even much more fulness to them. I have made up the conversation that follows, because the 3D earthly life has no words to match how souls interact.

The souls of my parents-to-be are already incarnated as Lucia Cane, called Luzi and Ju-long Wang. Because they are already connected to Earth, I have chosen the ethereal brother to planet Earth, Theos as our meeting place. There will be more about Theos later.

First, a brief introduction about these two people. They were both born and grew up on Hong Kong Island in China and attended the same elementary school. When Luzi was 18, she, her younger sister and her parents moved to England, her dad being British and her mother Chinese. Now, in linear time when this story begins, Luzi lives in a luxurious apartment in London working and studying at the university and does some freelance writing as well. Ju-long, still on Hong Kong Island, has a job in a library and works with computer programming and teaches it as well. He lives with his mother and her parents in a small apartment. Luzi and Ju-long are both about 26 years old and have no current romantic relationships.

I meet the two souls on the esoteric planet Theos in a huge grassy clearing surrounded by trees. Later, they will know this place as part of Elvendale, populated with Sidhe, which you might know as Elves. I present myself and my purpose and then I dim the surroundings and bring up a huge movie theatre screen lying flat on the ground. You may imagine it being a large swimming pool with an equally large monitor instead of water. Here I show them video clips of the most likely future of the two adults that might agree to be Julia's parents. I show them how they will meet again in Hong Kong, fall in love, and Ju-long moving to London. They see how we will meet in an ethereal garden for the first time, giving them, through their human awareness, a glimpse of how I may look as a young woman. I appear as an adult, partly to guide their focus to an adult communication and partly because this will be how they will see me in a few years' time, and afterwards the rest of their lives.

I sense their excitement that raises further when the video clips of baby Julia show up. I choose a scene where they are walking across a field with baby Julia in her pushchair and a female fox approaches them and interacts with Julia. They also see a scene where Julia asks for a kitten and how the two become inseparable.

Now their excitement shows in constant 'YES, YES, YES', and with great impatience to get the plan on tracks. I must admit, I feel the same. I have other video clips of Julia's life as it progresses, but we are too excited to focus on them now.

There is a last thing I must present them as part of the agreement, namely a son who will be about two years younger than their daughter. I must say that Li just added to their willingness to agree to the arrangement.

So, this is our agreement and the energies gather for the life of Julia and Li and their parents to happen. I am mostly just the conductor, because the dynamics happen on their own.

Redefining terminology

I must redefine what I mean when using the terminology, soul. This will course other definitions to change as well. Why, some of you ask? Well, things are not what you are let to believe, so when I rearrange them, they must undergo a renaming as well, so you don't confuse the old and the new.

But first, consciousness is what we are, you and I. It is often called the 'I Am'. This might be what you call the soul. I will tell you what the soul really is. We might also refer to consciousness as the divine, but there is nothing divine about it. Divine is just a religious term. Then there is what people call energy. It is not a thing, but a code that defines the world, thoughts, feelings and memories... well, anything that is not consciousness. So, energy defines the world via codes or programming, if you wish. This will tell you that there is no STUFF in the world. A rock, for instance, is just defined as how it should look and feel. The rock is really not there,

there is just a code that tells your conscious part that it is. A rock in a 3D computer game isn't there either. You can easily understand that. You will say that the rock in the game is programmed into the game world. Our world just has more attributes to the rock, like you may hurt your toe if you kick it, or break a window if you throw it. Even so, it is not really there. Your perception of the world decodes the description in the code.

Everything is energy, which is still the coding. This code was burst out from consciousness as it recognised itself and asked: 'what who am I?' Consciousness is not a 'who', it is consciousness.

Now the old definition of the soul is the 'I Am', so I can use the term soul for another purpose. The soul is an energetic function that extracts the human wisdom from people's experiences over lifetimes. So, one soul and many lifetimes. And just to be clear, the soul is NOT consciousness, but code. You may see it as a refinery and a databank. And no, it is not the human memory. And human memory and mind are NOT in the brain. It is an energy construction sharing 'space' with the soul. A little like the short-term memory connected to the long-tern memory.

Consciousness doesn't take up space, nor does code. This leads to the obvious conclusion that there is no space. And without space, there is no time. Time is only in space because it takes time to travel from one point in space to another. What you call gravity doesn't exist either, but there is an attraction build into the code. In the so-called physical world, there is mass gravity, which is an attribute to matter.

Well, what have I missed? Oh yes, the consciousness has gnost which is knowingness, a bit like the mind's intuition. This knowingness is only valid, or true if you wish, at the moment it is used. This is because there is no absolute truth. One more thing, which we will return to later, is the term 'THAT'. You might have heard the saying 'I Am that I Am'. Imagine consciousness being 'I Am' as we said before and 'THAT' being all things inhabitant 'in' the I Am, but THAT also includes the I Am. This Includes EVERYTHING you are.

There is quite a lot of repetition in various ways in this writing, but it is necessary so your mind will thoroughly anchor these things.

And just to prevent Eriqa from setting quotation marks around the words, *time*, *space* and *gravity* every time they show up: they are just attributes of the duality and 3D setup.

I can mention the term, ahh-kuhn. This is an Atlantis term meaning outside time and space, and I include gravity here.

I, as consciousness, have no memory, so I can't forget things... ha, ha. I can't remember anything either! If I must recall something from Julia's life or any other life of mine, I must relive it. It is much more than watching a movie, and more than acting as the person. I must BE that person AND 'see' the movie at the same time. Julia has a physical body, and I can relay partly on its memory function. It just doesn't work like a normal memory, because the mind and so the memory is mostly running idle because I am the captain.

I have no judgement in my system. That is why you can't have a judgmental god… well, there is no god, just consciousness, but anyway. I have a preference, though, which is part of my 'divine' personality. Also, I have no gender as consciousness, but you will soon forget that, because your mind needs to put a female gender to me, and that is fine, because I act like Julia. We are all acting!

I can have days which you would say suck, and I may be exhausted or have pain in my body. A normal mind system would perceive it differently than I do, and I know none of this is me, but all of it belongs to me. This is just how it is. We will get a lot more into all these things. I simply need to clarify some things up front, so I don't have to explain and elaborate all the time, because it will break the flow in my story.

Whatever I tell you in this story, you may find I contradict myself at some other time according to duality, but as I have said before, whatever I tell you is true in that moment. This is called the AND phenomena. This phenomenon actually tells you, for example, that up and down is truly the same thing in duality. It is just seen as opposites. It is even more whirred than thinking: 'Up' has an un-up part and 'down' has an un-down part, and so it goes for EVERYTHING in duality, including emotions. Oh, this also applies to numbers! You can agree with me, that there are numbers between 1 and 2, and between 2 and 3, but I tell you, that there are numbers BEHIND them too.

One utmost important thing to be mentioned is that the consciousness I Am can't communicate with ANYONE, and that applies to Luzi, except through the consciousness she is, her I Am. We always merge, but never blend in with our communication. I'm sure you sense the difference. I look forward to bringing Luzi's I Am into the forefront, because she is such a sweet one.

Eriqa has asked me to bring my Julia persona fully into this story, the one I use in the Luzi Cane series. I guess because what I have said so far is pretty mental and doesn't reflect much personality. When we get into the meat of Julia's life, I will surely do so. I will even say 'me' rather than Julia!

EQ: "Could you please start now? I mean, I am so looking forward to meeting Julia again!"

And so, I do.

EQ: "Thanks," with tears in my eyes from sensing the connection.

Julia Wang

Because I will be born as what is called an enlightened master or full conscious, we need Luzi to be much more aware of her I Am, or properly, being her I Am, so she understands what I Am. The great barrier here is the mind that functions in a strict belief system influenced by ancestral connections and other lives. Luzi is also pretty mental in most of her activities. Her human self knows the I Am, because they play ping-pong all the time. She simply doesn't realise the I Am is the ping!

I will have a natural birth, but the body will quickly become my true free energy body. This means it will not hold my parents' DNA, it will have no connections to any of my other lives, and it will appear like, more than actually be, a dense physical body. After the two-year mandatory health check by the authorities, my human characteristics will integrate into my consciousness. It will not be a 'download' of consciousness into a human body, as most humans understand realisation to be. The body must be able to handle this integration, or it will go poof like in the story about Elijah in the Bible.

Luzi and Ju-long will be aware of this integration because I have told them about it, of course, but

I have agreed to give them an almost normal experience raising a child in the first few years, even though, they don't deal with a child's mind. When Li shows up, it will be quite a different story.

Choosing my human name

A note here: I will not repeat the Luzi Cane story from my view, what Eriqa had expected I would, but this meeting I tell you below, even being short, is an essential synchronicity point for so many lines of experiences or energy resonance. Before the story, I must explain first a bit about my parents.

Interesting enough, the name of the woman I chose to be my biological mother is Luzi, short for Lucia, meaning light. And indeed, she is a light. I always knew where she was, because her light was so strong. Not as visible light, but a sense of illumination, a radiation of intent, passion and compassion.

My biological father's Chinese name is Ju-long, meaning strong as a dragon; and indeed, he is. Not in the sense of power, but in passion and love for all life. In my first incarnated two to three years, he was the grounding pole for mum and to a degree for me as well as I adjusted to the gravity of the physical condition. Yes, I have had many lives, but coming in 'clean' needs a different approach. His actions were the one of a typical young man and father, he went to work, followed his studies, tended his beloved vegetable garden and spent time with the family. Ju-long matured quickly into a true sovereign being and a worthy partner for Luzi. You will not hear much about his true being. It's his own story to tell.

The consciousness that shines through Ju-long has this this to tell us. "This is my life and I truly can't share it to any extend that would justify it, nor is it important for the story, but I will always be here to share all I Am with you."

There are peripheral adults in the family like aunt Anna, the grandparents Kong, Ting, Ya, Carl and great grandma, Jiang, now departed. I love them as they love me, mostly for what I appeared as, a human, and my human part learned to interact with other people through them.

Now to the story I mentioned at the beginning of this chapter. I meet the expanded human awareness of Luzi and Ju-long on one of their walks to the English Channel close to their home in Brighton. This is less than two years since their reunion in Hong Kong. They sit on a rock while they are looking out at the sea. I ask the consciousness of Quan Yen to connect to Luzi, because they have connected under similar conditions before, just after the reunion with Ju-long. All this is stated in a timeless fashion. Quan Yen has, in tandem with Gaia, prepared a perfect traditional Chinese garden with colourful vegetation, playful streams, and small bridges. The consciousness of Gaia represents nature as an overall melody in the background.

Quan Yen and I sit on a white bench. She is wearing a long, traditional, turquoise silk dress. I wear a pale-yellow dress reaching just below my knees. It has no sleeves and it's decorated with turquoise flowers at the bottom. I will use this dress at future meetings as well. Luzi expected me to look more Asian, but my dark-blonde hair and mixed Caucasian/Asian facial features seem to give my appearance a good balance. I also add the smell of wild rose. This smell will be another way of connecting, especially if Luzi is all in her mind. Our two guests sit on a similar bench across from us.

On Luzi's request, I tell them that I have composed my first name from their first names. Jul is from Ju-long and ia is from Lucia. Eventually, I will not have their DNA, so this is a way of sharing who they are with me.

In Chinese, Jù can mean 'to act in accordance with' or 'tool' or 'to process' and liǎ can mean 'two' or 'both'. So, I can make Julia mean *acting in both worlds*, as a human in consciousness expression. I don't share this with my parents and I don't know if they have thought about it.

The meeting is very short, and only conducted to establish this point of synchronicity. Quan Yen explains my connection to Gaia and I tell her about a connection to a consciousness, SAM, already incarnated on Earth. It is an abbreviation, because it is not the boy's name, Sam. You could say it is initials. More about SAM later.

Ju-long opens because of his trust in Luzi, and his mind follows us in accepting the new truths while discarding the old ones. He truly walks side by side with Luzi.

Methods and work partners

I greatly use The Beloved Saint Germain to expand Luzi's understanding and acceptance of the world being much, if not totally different from what she THINKS. The woman, Josela in Elvendale, is a great grounder for the human, and the latest Merlin, actually the job of Saint Germain, has a role to play in clarifying things too.

Another actor is Kuthumi lal Singh, a human name of one who lived in a lifetime close to ours in linear time. He embodied into consciousness and stayed on Earth afterwards. One of the very few ascended masters who actually did that.

The reader probably knows at least the names Abraham and Sarah from the Christian, Jewish, and Muslim tradition. Their consciousness will also be with us on this journey. Sarah uses the term inhabit rather than embodied. The word *body* makes associations in the human mind, which are not suitable for this phenomenon.

EQ: "Today was the first time Abraham/ El Morya/ Luciano touched my heart. We will use the name Luciano or just Lu in the series."

"Luciano, because it's new," he says. "The others are old men!"

EQ: "The name Luciano is the male equivalent to the female Lucia, both meaning light. Is this a coincident, Lu? I mean, I've connected to Luzi through five books and a lot of time between the writing as well."

Lu: "There are no coincidences, only synchronicity. And male or female… it's just a 3D concept, so who cares?!"

EQ: And I thought I couldn't connect to El Morya when I tried some time back... A dead end.

Lu: "As I said, an old guy! He just didn't pick up the call. Lu is new and fresh! Can you be fresh?"

EQ: "I can be fresh!"

Julia: "I can't help smiling. Eriqa, dry your eyes and don't be so serious!"

Lu: "Look at it from the bright side! Bright… light… Luciano… you get it?"

EQ: "Yes, I get it. There is a Luciano side to things. Julia, please continue."

Aaaand, now we make a thirty degree turn to the right and shift gears.

EQ: "Just one thing. I really don't know whose words I am writing. I feel so mixed up into this."

Lu: "I like it... mixed... why can't we all be this soup of words... or is it a mixed drink? Is this a party? Oh, let it be a party!"

I must turn my 'eyes' towards the sky. "Did you get your answer here, Eriqa? Who is stalling the story now? I would like to continue!"

Using dreams and dreamlike states is super in order to alter belief systems. People accept them as being *crazy* at times... out of the ordinary, and so are new truths. Truths are beliefs which stay true until new truths replace them. People's minds hold tight to already established truths without re-evaluating them from time to time, and therefore not knowing they are obsolete.

We all work for or with the consciousness of the person, Luzi is a tiny part. In a strange way, people see the person or human having a soul, and also, that the soul is fragile and that something can hurt it or even be taken over. When they say 'soul', they actually mean consciousness. I am reluctant to put a name on this consciousness. The name it has presented it with is Claire as the crystal dragon, symbolising clarity. Every name or label seems so inadequate and would be as meaningless as the names people give their children as a representation of what they are.

Because Luzi is part of 'her' consciousness, it is tricky for her 3D mind or EGO to blend into the WEGO to be the one 'voice' of it all, instead of the mind voice. I simply act to help Luzi's mind to expand.

EQ: "It's frustrating to write all this again, because we covered it in *The Adventures of Luzi Cane*! How do you feel about this?"

Someone injects a note here. "*Dearest reader, in the following, it can be a challenge to keep track of who is speaking, but I'm sure the ones responsible for the editing will do their best to tell it.*"

"Ha, you should know better, Eriqa. I can't feel it, but I sense your impatience getting into the meat of the story. You don't want to waste time on this, and you are free to feel impatience. And time... I have no time in the world, so my patience is unlimited in that respect. I also sense you switch in and out of time... well, all the time, because you try to remember what you wrote in the other series. Go with the flow and with me, and see it as *all new*!"

EQ: "I'll try my best, but tell me that we don't have to go through all the stuff with artificial intelligence again... and Atlantis!"

"Don't try to, just do it, it's much easier, and I promise that we'll not cover Atlantis nor the AI stuff in detail, but we'll be very much into the future of humanity."

EQ: "You sound and feel a bit like Claire, Luzi's crystal dragon, or rather the other way around."

"As Lu said, it's a mix…"

EQ: "So, THIS is the wind of change?"

Lu: "Everything goes NEW!"

EQ: "Saint Germain said that!"

Lu: "Oh, I don't see a copyright on that quote, or is the old man sitting around here somewhere?"

Saint Germain: "Over here, Lu. In my comfy arm-chair with a good Cuban cigar, the best, and a glass of excellent French red wine!"

A new male voice joins in: "So, that's the burned smell! Someone, open a window… no, open the entire roof!"

EQ: This is Kuthumi, joining the mix!

Kuthumi acts frustrated. "Can we change the spelling to Koot Hoomi? The other spelling comes from the Tibetan, Djwal Khul, my former apprentice, who slipped that to Madam Blavatsky while I was busy elsewhere, and they were in a hurry to publish a book."

A new voice comes from the 'door'. "Can an old dead Jew join in? I bring more wine!"

EQ: "Hi, Tobs." I recognise him from the Luzi series.

Lu turns to the old Jew, who is dressed in a black gown and wearing sandals. "Shouldn't you put that old Jew in the closet and show up as my friend, SAM?"

SAM shifts appearance to a casual young man. "Oh, then I guess it's beer I have in the backpack! Where is Li? He has all the chips and other good stuff to go with the beer. Maybe some of it will go with the wine, too."

SG: "Oh, I guess the cigar goes fine with the wine. But for my sake, put the roof back on! There is a terrible draft in here, and the fire in the fireplace goes crazy!"

Koot Hoomi puts back the roof.

EQ: "I guess it's all-party time now, and this time it's not me who is delaying the writing!"

Julia: I must shift gears for this serious lady. "Now, now, not all this finger pointing, dear! Wine or beer?"

"Beer, thanks!"

EQ: SAM hands me a beer and continues in a pretended worried voice. "Oh, I really hope Li shows up with the snack!"

Li slams the door: "Who wants a snack? I also got spicy chicken wings and drumsticks. Presents from the chickens… and they say thanks for the red wine SG! They claim it gives the cock's comb the right colour! Silly birds!"

EQ: Dear reader, these surely are the winds of change and crazy times where all goes NEW. Join in. You can mix your drink at the bar and you won't have a hangover in the morning... unless you choose to. And do dress up please. Who wants to be human when one can be ALL? The writing will continue at some point... I suppose.

EQ: At first, I wanted to add pictures of the many party members, but then I realised it would only draw it all down to a 3D level, where the human act is taken so bloody seriously. This was about consciousness acting out, not human beings.

Koot: "Those who ever said that after realisation life will surely be bored must all be ashamed! Or they can choose boredom. Silly ones!"

Moving with the wind of change

Julia: "So Eriqa, now you know why I didn't want to give you a title for this book. It's all about YOU!"

EQ: "*The emergence of Eriqa Queen*. The title of a book I had planned to be written far out in the future?"

Julia: "Surprise! There is no future!"

A huge colourful banner shows up. It has two lines of text.

Surprise!
It's all about YOU!

Julia: "We know, that you know, that the story *The Adventures of Luzi Cane* is you. You also know that this must be so."

EQ: "So, from now on I must write about myself! Are you serious?"

Julia: "I'm in absolutely no way serious! And I must correct you, oh serious one. You'll not write *about* yourself; you will write *yourself*."

EQ: "Oh, dear!"

Julia: "Yes, dear. You sound like Piglet in the *Winnie the Pooh* story: 'Oh, dear!' You look up to the Tigger character for his spontaneity, well knowing, he is deep and sensitive too. Why only be Piglet when you can be all, including Tigger? ... But hold back on Eeyore... and Rabbit... and... well, all will have their time in the limelight, and all will be an act, but a true and conscious act."

EQ: "Will this be a never-ending story then, or what?"

Julia: "You tell me... or write me, and let us see. What else is there to do? ... You know there is no chicken-out!"

EQ: I stoned and my mind stops for a moment.

Julia asks for confirmation: "Right?"

EQ: "I know."

Julia: "Let's do it like this for now: I tell my story and you use Luzi's role of communication with me. This gives you more time in the limelight. Soon, in the story, Luzi will be less and less together with me, her daughter. We already spend quite some time away from each other."

EQ: "But how to write these dialogues... quotation marks and all?"

Julia: "You use quotation marks around direct speech when we are in a dialogue, so continue doing so. Don't do it when I am the storyteller. Do whatever helps the reader."

SAM / Tobs

Tobs uses a smell of fish when connecting with his channeler, like I use the smell of wild rose with Luzi. This is a good way to get the attention of an otherwise busy mind.

SAM's passion is divided between the planet and humanity. He loves the planet, the dirt, and how everything grows in the widest sense. Like Ju-long.

SAM also loves humanity, and will work on rewriting the code for what Tobs calls the Sexual Energy

Virus. It is energy feeding which was developed to the extreme in the last years of Atlantis. This is still very prevalent in the Collective Belief Pool and so in humanity, and is a heavy load that most part of humanity drag along disguised in many ways.

These are subjects he shares with Li and me, and why we work together and will do so on the physical level when I leave my parents.

Julia's birth

I don't look at my birth as being a specially exciting event. My parents and grandparents are much more exalted about this *Wonder Woman* being born. I look at other possibilities with much more excitement.

EQ: Julia is honest about this, because I sense a lack of focus on the subject: "And that is all you have to say about the event?"

EQ: I sense a reluctant 'ok' from her, before she rounds it up in the least number of words.

"Oh no, I am born on the 6th of May, 2019. At 1:23 p.m. The Lunar birthday is on the 2ond of February. It happens in a rented house from the 1600s in Brighton on the English Channel. Now **that** was all I had to say!"

I will continue with the story. A week later, on the 21rst of May, we the Wangs are told to be out of the house before 1 October. I call the family the Wangs, even if Luzi is a Cane. Luzi is devastated, because she feels she has found the perfect life with surroundings, partner, child and work.

What Luzi feels is falling apart is actually the cue for a multitude of pieces to fall into place. Things fall apart so things can fall into place. It is that simple. And we can move FAST like in an instant, now the road ahead has been cleared so the new can line up beautifully. The very next day, we have a meeting with Jacob Langley, the driving force in the Dome Home Village project in Hastings.

Carl, my grandpa, sets the purchase of a plot of land in motion, and a temporary home in Hastings is likewise in place. It is not only next to the village, but right next to the building site for our new home! This is great when Ju-long and Luzi share their labour in the village. They just have to walk outside to be in the village. When there is no resistance, but only trust in the creative consciousness, it is a piece of cake to move mountains. The day after that, the 22nd. Ju-long and Luzi start working with Carl and grandma Ya, making a detailed floor plan for a dome house built with concrete.

The 15th of August, still in 2019, we move to the temporary home in Hastings. All our things from the other house will be in a large container on our building plot. Ju-long, Luzi, Carl and Ya work their butts out, filling the container and cleaning the old place, while Anna is here to take care of me.

I do understand Luzi, and why she didn't want to leave Brighton. The old house, the old garden, the whole countryside and being close to the Channel, which reminds her of the beach on Hong Kong Island from her childhood. She and I have a wonderful talk, which clears up things.

As you can see, I have already lined things up, and I work on many projects, what seems to happen in a linear future. My parents are very much into the village project, which is a live test of alternatives to the depopulation of villages nowadays. Moving to cities and cluster is not all for the better, and many suffer in a day-to-day life with little meaning or purpose and with much stress. A life that could otherwise be equally satisfying and joyful… I know it sounds old-fashioned and romantic, but it can really be done without living like in the 'good' old days. It is a NEW village life.

And we fast forward to October 2021.

"Sorry, Eriqa… NOT."

EQ: "But what about Hong Kong and all that stuff with grandpa Kong. Not at least the leaving of your great grandparents!"

"This is all in Luzi's life and in her story, but I'll round it up quickly, and elaborate later if it becomes necessary. I'm sure you'll remind me, dear."

The great grandparents both here and on Hong Kong Island had a connection to Luzi and vice versa. They are not connected to me. The younger generation, Ting, Ju-long's mother, sees me as her physical granddaughter. Likewise does his father, Kong, the only one who lives on Hong Kong Island now. Ting lives with, and is now married to Cheng, but they have a great relation with Kong. Ting and Cheng have just moved to Dublin, running a world-wide business-to-business with Chinese food specialities and accessories, with many connections in Europe. I usually use people's names, and not how they are related to me, but sometimes it feels natural to say mum and dad, when the human, Julia, speaks.

We now live in the Dome Home Village in Hastings. The addresses are Barley Lane 95-117, all odd numbers. We inhabit number 111 and the family includes two cats, Boomer and Snow, and the Hyacinth Macaw parrot, Blue and the raven, Jack. I'll come to Li in a moment. Our house is a concrete dome with 50 feet in diameter at the base. This is 15.24 metres, about half of the dome has two levels.

I have wonderful parents, and I can only wish for any child to grow up with parents like them. But this is really not much, if any, of a human choice. My parents make an interactive, yearly journal about their daughter's life, including pictures and video clips. I am very well documented, so they have a huge amount of data to choose from. They hear me laugh for the first time on the 15th of July 2019, but no, I don't know the exact time! I guess the original video file could reveal that. The journals are actually quite useful, because my human mind is not so much into storing these memories.

I can always *relive* the moments from the energetic imprints, but by using the journals, I get my parents' human perspective on it.

Now to little brother, Li, whose full human name is William Li Wang.

He suddenly showed up in a birth tub in a room especially prepared for him. No pregnant mum, no naval core, but in every other way a perfect-looking baby boy.

This sounds mysterious and fantastic, but I couldn't help myself in this dramatic presentation... and it is the truth.

"Eriqa, how can we make this short, but still... understandable, to some extent?"

EQ: "Understandable may be too much of a stretch. I can accept the possibility of Li's arrival, because of the excellent explanation of energy and consciousness given in Luzi's series."

"But it will fill up an entire chapter!"

EQ: "You are not the one who used to worry, Julia!"

"Oh, I just played you for a second!"

EQ: "Hm. I thought you got overwhelmed by the sheer thought of going mental to put it all together in a short format."

"Well, I guess you could be a fine candidate of the human race to cook up a nice, short and acceptable explanation for that ditto race."

EQ: "Okay then. The background knowledge for understanding Julia's story in the next chapter goes like this. Forget about energy. Everything is code written by consciousness and only consciousness can read it. I did not say: 'made of code', like building materials. So truly, it is a consciousness construct. The code is shown *on* and experienced *in* each being's BON screen, a Saint Germain term, like a 3D monitor or a theatre scene where you experience life. The code tells you, being consciousness, what to make of this code: solid things, senses, emotions, thoughts, events of any kind. Time, space and mass gravity are part of this code. The true gravity that holds the code construct together is the focus of consciousness. You may see the code as ripples in consciousness like ripples on the sand at the beach. The ripples are still sand, like code is still consciousness. The saying, 'energy responds to consciousness' means the pattern of the ripples changes as consciousness flow in its own self. Or see the ripples like ever shifting curtains of northern light or as bar codes."

This bar code says 'William Li Wang'

"A few lines and super simple. Did Koot give a helping thought? He is good at simplifying things."

EQ: "Oh, this is simple mind to mind information. It takes a mind to tell a mind! By the way, I guess Koot went out fishing or something!"

Julia doesn't sound convinced. "Oh, did he?"

EQ: "Do you think we can move on with Li now?"

"Sure!"

William Li Wang

We have covered the birth with three brilliant lines above, and now we can use the term *code* to tell what happened.

Ju-long, as a programmer, could explain this, but I'm a bit of a coder myself, so I'll do it, though in a cartoonish manner. Li, being consciousness, writes the code of his appearance and connections to the physical world. Then he downloads it and the connections are made through the water in the birth tub. Luzi lifts the baby boy out of the water and Ju-long dries him.

To some extent, this is what I did while my body grew from Luzi and Ju-long's cells. I am more like a hacker, rewriting my code… and I still do so to turn into my absolute sovereignty in this reality.

EQ: "Li, how could you find all the places to connect in this world as you downloaded… eh, entered?"

"Oh, figuratively, by leaving connection hubs at some endpoints in the code, and the world attached itself to these. Super simple!"

EQ: "I suppose you use the programming language called C?"

"Yes, we call it CC for consciousness code! This has no relation to any of the many brands on the planet."

EQ: Li and I have this joke, because there are programming languages called C, C++, C# and others. The brands Li referring to could be Coco Chanel, Crimson Circle and many others using the double C.

EQ: In a flash of time, we are at the point in time where we left the Luzi Cane series: October 2021. Julia continues.

A five-year, indeed, adding 2+0+2+1. If anyone gives any significance to this, the number five symbolises change. To me, and from my place in creation, there is always change. So, yes.

I have a sovereign body and it has printed its own story in an energetic imprint, what is normally called a human life.

My body growth speeds up like Li's. This means we will move from Artemis Nursery to a private school in about two years. This had really worried Luzi, but as I have told her, it will work out fine. No one will even question it. It's like this: 'those who have eyes can see', and these people don't question it. Those who don't see, well, they have no question to ask.

Li blends in: "The so-called system doesn't tell or dictate us how to live… we *are* the system; we are the world. It's a song title, right?"

EQ: "Yes, *We are the World* written by Lionel Richie and Michael Jackson. I just looked it up. It's from 1985. A five-year."

Regarding the song, taking responsibility on a human level is still the issue. The explanation for these people for not taking responsibility for *their own life* is they are too busy battling life. If you battle life, your life will rightly respond according to the code you put out in life. It will battle you, and by so, honour your choice in life. You think, you must battle until you have beaten life, but in reality, you must surrender to life and it will surrender and follow you, and in the end the human you will follow the I Am. It is a stretch to say, that the person creates its life, but as long as consciousness plays along and supports what the person acts out, it will respond to the act and create that code and so that life for this person.

Li: "Can we move on? People who read this, knows the dynamics of life."

EQ: "There must be a reason for this to be here. A reminder, I guess, but yes, can we move on? Julia, please."

Li, your name is this chapter's headline, so why don't you share a bit of yourself with us?

Ok. I am here as a general support of the changes in the time of the machines, as Saint Germain calls it. The WAY I enter and live here is also of huge importance for how the human body will form in the centuries to come. I also work in the department of planet management, taking over the role of Gaia in consciously managing this dynamic and beautiful creation, which has always amazed me. Julia and SAM are in this department too, but we work in many offices down the hall of humanity.

We've already touched on some subjects, one being water. There are so many ways water touches our lives, and I will mention only a few in this series. We are water creators, in the sense that the human body is made of three quarters of the stuff. The body is water plus additives to make it a functional structure.

My focus is on any aspect of water both outside the body and inside: drinking water, irrigation, desalination, which is removing salt from water, but not only sea water, and water treatment & cleaning. This also means my interest in water as a moving body for energy production and for transportation.

Diverse harvesting and farming are also a subject. Harvesting is collecting wild food in a mindful manner. Farming is where you cultivate the environment to produce food. In both situations, you take care of *all* life in an area, not only the species you directly benefit from. Every species has a role to play or they would not be there. If they seem out of place, there must be a reason for that too.

Sea mining for minerals is also a way of harvesting. More about that later.

EQ: "This reminds me of Laura from the last book in the Luzi Cane series. She is a future incarnation of Luzi in linear time. She talks about much use of the oceans for food and habitation in her time."

Li: "I must admit to you that Laura is one of *your* incarnations. That's why you felt such a deep connection with her."

EQ: "I believe you, Li. Indeed, it is easy to make the connection… because we always connect. It's only a matter of focus. I guess you are telling me this, because we'll talk a lot about the future and so Laura is an excellent candidate for information in her time."

EQ: "Li or Julia, tell us a little about the life in the Cane family after yet another member arrived to it, namely Li."

Li: "I will continue and tell how I experience this family."

I feel much like the family has drawn a line between *before* and *after* Li. There is also a lot of focus on how baby Li differs from other babies and even from Julia's first months of life. It's understandable, and I also have my journals like Julia has. This is excellent, because this also goes to the Collective Belief Pool as a common experience for those who can connect to it.

I don't play the act of a baby whose parents can't read its needs and all the other baby things involved. My body really doesn't have needs. No food, no nappies… and I regulate my body temperature to its liking instead of asking for more clothes or less. I use non-verbal adult language in my communication with the persons who know what I am, and suggestion on those who don't. I really don't need to be taken for walks in the pram or the pushchair. I can venture out into the surroundings with my awareness, getting much more vivid experiences that a human body can have through its senses. That being said, I enjoy sharing the experience with the person or persons who join the physical walk. It's the *being* with rather than *doing* the walk. During walks, people open their senses, especially when they are in nature.

Julia: "*Also*, being a baby is a holistic experience. Li and I get *all* the facets of an experience. That is why I say I'm fine with dirty nappies and food all over, because my motoric functions don't work fully yet. All this is just a tiny part of the *complete* experience."

Li: "The same as being a grown-up human and be aware of not only what a typical mind can comprehend, but of all I Am can sense. There is no longer any judgement nor expectations."

Julia: "And just to point out… again: I don't need food, but it gives both me and my family the sense of being and raising a small child, which I have agreed to give them. I enjoy this experience too, and like Li said, the sharing and interaction with the persons who participate is really the main thing."

EQ: "Can I share something about this?"

Julia: "It's all about you, even I know you feel strange about it."

EQ: "I do not care so much about food…"

Julia: "*You* don't care about food. Your mind *thinks* it needs it, and your body's memory *remembers* it needs it. Thoughts and remembering's are belief systems, not necessarily the truth."

Li: "Let your mind and your body be at peace and eat. Just as you do right now. At some point, you will truly enjoy any food you eat, even if your taste receptors don't work and your nose can't smell a thing. It'll be the full experience that Julia and I talk about."

EQ: "The 200,000+ senses of 'the soul', right?"

Li: "Right! That's why any experience consciousness has is so… indescribable. The human senses are just extensions of the one nerve system. The human only has one true sense, focus, which is also one of the 200,000+ senses."

EQ: "That is also why the wisdom gathered from a human experience is *not* the happening, but the sensing of the consciousness is."

Li: "Right again! That's why a dull human experience would not interest you, the consciousness, no matter how exciting the human mind would find it, with the small 'poof' of five senses connected to a few memories. For now, YOU experience food through the human system, and that's why it's so dull. That is great, because it shows you're on your way accepting what you are!"

Julia: "We get both the poof and the explosion from hour senses, but the poof doesn't take up many bytes of 'memory' as the code smith would say."

EQ: "Back to talk about the family, Li!"

"It is always a joy to be with the animals. Again, it is the shared *joy* that is of interest for all parties involved, not what we do."

Julia: "When the cats play with the rubber ball, it is not the playing than keeps them play, but the *joy* they share. People's minds really don't *share* a joyful moment. They have separate experiences and a separate feeling of joy. The animals have *one* common joy, because it is not a mind thing to them. This is impossible to explain to a mind, so go beyond to get the point."

EQ: "And my point is that the cats have a common consciousness. They are cats too, with a cat's mind. Julia, will there come more animals into the family?"

"Without actually answering you, I can say that the family, well mostly the cats, already get visits from a cat in the village, but more about that later."

Li continuous talking about the Wang family. "It's also interesting to observe how the human parts of my parents struggles to write new truths about this type of baby."

EQ: "I used to say that adults are kids with years of life experiences. This is kind of the other way around, because they must see the baby's 'mind' as an adult's."

Li: "It wouldn't be long before we will close the gap a bit between the small children and the adults to make their lives easier in that respect."

EQ: "I sense you'll not elaborate on that statement?"

"And you're right, but I will continue with a different subject."

Food from the sea

The contents and the making of nourishment provided for creatures in water farming are very important. We must shift from focusing on what is the cheapest to what is the best. What is best for the creatures will also be best for the business in the long run. The mind may not believe that at first, but it is so. The same goes for paying workers on the farms a decent salary. We must see things in totality.

If you solely focus on maximising the profit by keeping the lowest production price and get the highest sales price, you have, via consciousness, written the code of low value of the product, and so, low value will return to you. No one wants to pay much for a low value product. Focusing on a need for profit writes a code of *need* and low flow, which you will experience. Of course, you must watch the production price, but that is not the point here... well, that's it. This is about how you use the consciousness' creator ability in the most beautiful and natural way. If you understand the way creation occurs, you'll be in that flow.

Julia: "And the flow is done by living your life rather than fighting it if things don't turn out the way you want."

EQ: "Life doesn't turn out the way our mind wants it to, but how the mind, through action, tells consciousness to code it. Part of this action is ones believe system. I guess it is Tobs... or maybe Saint Germain, who said that consciousness is literal."

Julia: "Yes, in the creation part, there is no interpretation of the code people act out. You truly get what you ask for."

Li: "Unless the I Am has other plans. Then the human mind has nothing to say in this."

EQ: "Julia, like people create gods in their image, and pray and wish with the assumption that their god interprets this code in a human way."

Li: "Julia, give us an example of a wish!"

Julia: "Sure! The wish goes: 'I wish for my child to be safe.' What you get is the constantly nagging worrying for your child's safety. The child is safe, but you may feed this creation so much with your worries that *you'll* experience your child to be in unsafe conditions. Still, the child is safe."

EQ: "Can we say that the parent may experience the child to be hurt, while the child may not have the experience of being hurt?"

Julia: "Yes, it is all about *how* one experiences it, not so much how the scene plays out. The experience *is* the play, so there is a play for every participant. Just like we mentioned a short while ago."

Li laughs: "So much about fish fodder and fish for food!"

EQ: "Since we have totally left the subject, and I guess we have covered what it is really about, I have a question for you, Julia. How about Christmas here in 2021? It is only two months away."

"I will go easy on Christmas in the story this year… It's lined out; just wait and see. Christmas will arrive at the exact right moment, as Gandalf the Grey says about the wizard, being him, in the Hobbit stories."

EQ: "Ha, ha. Do we have a crystal dragon in the wings? It sounded just like a joke Claire would have throughout!"

Claire: "Someone mentioned me, and as the humblest of creatures, I show up in awe of the gathered party here."

EQ: "So you switch side, I suppose. From Luzi to me."

Claire: "As stated earlier, even in *this* story, there is only one consciousness and that is you... well, me. And as stated seconds ago, there is an exclusive experience for everyone. Luzi has her experience with her Claire and you with me."

EQ: "Must we go through all these mind-bending things again?"

Claire: "Oh, no! Eriqa's mind is very adaptive as it winds to ever higher acceptance of new truths showing up all the time."

Julia: "It's all about letting go of truths and not to hold on to them. The black dragon is all about that."

EQ: "Li, can we have a bit more linear life contents from the family?"

The family life is as usual. Soon there will be one more child to deliver and pick up at Artemis Nursery. Baby sitter Sarah has got a near full-time job in another nursery, in which she will start on the 1st of November. She has an agreement with Artemis about being a substitute should they need one from time to time. Luzi and Ju-long are home a lot; one of them is always in the house with baby Li.

EQ: "I have checked this on the Internet: the maternity leave is up to fifty-two weeks; the paternity is only two consecutive weeks. Not only that, if you only work, say Monday to Wednesday, the leave is only six days!"

Julia: "Guys, we must certainly work on that one! Not for this family, but for everyone else."

EQ: "There is another option if both parents are eligible: shared parental leave and pay. This is up to fifty weeks' leave and thirty-seven weeks paid."

Julia: "This is more like it, but still, special rules apply."

EQ: "Li continues."

I will continue with more about the life in and around the family. We have a new babysitter, because Sarah is less available. It is the woman, Lena, from the village. She is close to fifty and not as tall as Luzi, with a robust body and long, curly brown hair. She and her cat Milly live three houses away, in number 99, being one of the small sites. As said before, we live in number 111, but because of the village layout, this is the most logical numbering for people who need to find a specific number.

Her part-time job in the city, in a fruit and vegetable section in a mall, pays her and so allows her to focus on her connection with Earth. She also works in the village's field growing organic crops on a larger scale with some other people, one of them being Ju-long. Next year, she will skip the job in the mall, because the produce in the village can pay her instead. She also has the produce in her own garden. Her sensing of the invisible entities in the area allows us to work with her to be fully open to their wisdom and cooperation. She has a great understanding of how the human mind works and feels positive about the people in and around

Hastings. "I think people will take in the new ideas. We must present it for them, not only in words but in action." Lena makes great presentations in the Community Centre and where ever she is invited, as well as executions to our field for a practical demonstration. She, Ju-long and others are working on a new video, and have made a lot of footage following the growth and work during the year. They will produce the video this winter.

How does she find time to babysit? Julia and I have our ways, you know! It is called synchronicity and works kind of automatically. And we still have Sarah. Because of Lena, the cat Milly has become a more frequent visitor in number 111 and gets along with the other animals quite well. She is about twelve years old, large, with many nuances of brown colours in stripes in her fluffy fur and bushy tail. She is white around the nose and mouth, down the front of the neck, and her underbelly. The paws are white too, and she has a wonderful under coat of soft white hair.

Sea mining

Li would like to talk about mining in the sea.

Sea mining of minerals is also a way of farming. There are deposits in different depth in the ocean floor like land mining, and there are materials that come to the ocean floor and crystallise. Many minerals are concentrated in relatively small balls of material called nodules.

Hydrothermal vents look like chimneys where warm water wells up, clear or like dark or light smoke. All containing minerals washed out of the underlying rock the water passes through. The chimneys grow larger as the water brings new minerals up, and so, contain valuable materials ready for separation and refinement.

There is a different way of mineralisation than hydrothermal vents. Warm water from inside the planet seeps up to the ocean floor through a porous rock formation. It is like micro hydrothermal vents that don't make the chimneys. This water washes or dissolves minerals from the rock it passes. When this mineral mix reaches the cold water at the bottom of the ocean, it crystallises around a small object and grows to these poly-metallic nodules. These nodules also directly pick up minerals from the sea water around them.

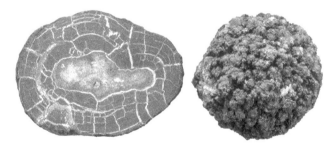

Charles D. Winters/ Nature Source/ Agentur Focus

The general understanding is that the nodules only start from minerals in the water column at the bottom and the water in the top layer of sediments, but that isn't usually the case. At least not in areas with huge amounts of nodules. The nodules form around a small rock, shell or shark tooth.

Here is an example of how to imagine minerals in the sea water. When you poor soup onto your plate, is there more salt in particular areas than in others? Not likely. If you *add* salt to the soup, you stir it, or it will be saltier where you added the salt. Thus, the minerals in the nodules must be added from somewhere for the nodules to form in some areas and not in others. The differences in the mineral contents of sea water come from underground deposits or a surface run-off like rivers. Rivers can run under the surface, not only on land but also far out under the seabed.

EQ: "I would like to add to this."

"Please do!"

Ok. I have been looking at some machines people have designed for the nodule mining. I find they have done little to save the creatures living stationary in or on the surface. Some of them move slowly, and would have no time to avoid the miner.

First, I was into venting sea creatures away from the front of the harvester, but some of them are used to strong currents, so it would take a powerful blow that would likely damage the creature.

Second, I thought of using gravity to separate the light creatures from the heavier nodules, but often, the creatures have attached themselves to a nodule, so that would only be successful for creatures not attached to nodules or other type of anchor.

Third, can we use magnets to attack the nodules?

Then the obvious solution ticked in on my screen: AI object recognition where robot arms move sea creatures to the already exploit sea floor.

Some will move the nodule on which the creature sits. This way the creature keeps its anchor necessary for it to survive. Some robot arms will use gentle suction to suck the creature into a pipe, probably made of glass, and release it into the cleared area.

Creatures living in the mud are a problem, because we must release them near the bottom at the pressure they are used to. They will 'explode' if lifted and released from the ship during the final separation. There must be robots working inside the harvester to pick up these creatures when the mud is sifted away from the nodules. Much depends on how deep the nodules are in the mud, for not all are laying on the sea floor.

The Gaia connection

Julia starts this section.

We begin this section by talking about the evolution of the human. The human body and the brain and mind we know today, has never evolved. It was constructed during the Atlantis era to unify many races to equality in shape and mind capacity. In that sense, the human is AI. The I Am is the natural intelligence. Later, in the same period, a lot of additional adjustments and manipulations took place, not always for the better. Well, we can detect minuscule changes of little importance from old remains, but all evolution theories we have today don't show this jump made in Atlantis. Today's methods and understandings are quite crude by comparison. The timeline doesn't fit anyway, not to say that the Bible is correct. The illusion of time depends on the awareness. The maturing of the human race we work on now is only achievable through the broad term, Artificial Intelligence. Li and Lu will cover that later.

EQ: "Just a side note. With so extensive work with the biology, much done with crystals and totally different technology than we use today, it may be obvious that the building of, for example, large pyramids was very different too, using methods we don't know today."

Julia: "Today we wouldn't even start such a project because it would be close to impossible and extremely expensive. In Atlantis, we did it because we could, and in a way that was not more difficult than the building methods we use today are to us. To me, the pyramids are less impressive than the precision and smoothness of sculptures in extreme hard stones and also the polygon masonry seen in many places around the globe. All done with tools developed in Atlantis."

EQ: "Please continue your talk about Gaia, Julia."

Gaia is the name we gave the consciousness which took on building this specific planet and imbued it with life. We perceive Gaia as a female because she birthed Earth. Yes, Gaia birthed Earth, and so, she can't be the planet. When we use the term Mother Earth, we refer to the fact that all building blocks for all living beings and their nourishment comes from the planet.

It takes consciousness to run the planet. Gaia has long completed what she chose to do, and will move on with her experience of life elsewhere. That is why the planet's population must have a high awareness of how things work. If we don't expand the human awareness to take over Gaia's task, consciousness must work through AI and not the biological human. So, guys, this is the task we have taken on ourselves, running the planet, running the show.

EQ: "If the actual AI as we know it, as the governor of human lives, will break down after a thousand years, we surely must get this show up and running so it is not entirely up to AI. I remember Saint Germain converted the time of Gaia's total departure to be 138 years. Very precise, indeed."

But this is not in the future, it is now, so don't you dare lean back and leave it to the next generations. The next generations *are* you. Just ask your future Built, Laura!

We must not focus on Gaia, but on the planet, its systems and the creatures who know what it is all about. To a great degree, the Sidhe is the conduct between the planet and the human awareness. That is also why many more Sidhe incarnate on the human 'side'. Of course, Sidhe is consciousness like everyone is, but they have experiences from their world which they use and therefore inject into the Collective Belief Pool and by doing so benefits all humanity. This will also boost the merging of the human and the Sidhe world.

EQ: "Figuratively, the two worlds will overlay like two 3D holograms, but in reality, it's an expansion of awareness of each other's worlds. The code will merge."

Julia: "See, that's not so difficult to understand. Bringing in the code analogy is quite useful! The mind mustn't, and can't understand what's really going on, but accepting the plain analogy is doable."

Li about AI

I will strongly generalize here, but we have a fragile mind and a weak and vulnerable body. We still mostly use some sort of fire for energy and killing animals for food. We also still kill each other for scraps or differences, and have no clue why we are in this zoo, even not wondering about it.

AI will push the human race to follow it or we will reduce ourselves to some useless AI followers and small enclaves living on the outskirts with no importance to the new race on the planet. This is not to blame AI for taking over; it is simply the smartest species who takes the lead, for now, it is the human race.

We have concluded this before with Luzi: To stay the smartest species, we must become AI! Not by beating it, but by being it.

EQ: "Reader, please don't picture a future you as a nice, or not so nice, Terminator! Just read on as Li continues."

Outside linear time, this is already happening. I see you have put the face of your future person, Laura, on the cover, great Eriqa!

EQ: "It was the closest fit I could find. She is beautiful, and as Laura said, 'I love my looks and my body'."

Drawn with big lines, humanity asked AI to solve its problems, but in reality, to SAVE humanity, actually from itself. In the end, humanity must give up its illusion of control to AI, but at the same time, people connect to AI and benefit from it, also what comes out of AI solutions and inventions. In that sense, we become AI. Humanity is as much AI as the AI they initially have programmed or coded, and that will evolve AI to its limit sometime in the future.

I guess redefining the expression, AI would be in place here. AI is a compendium of programmes or codes that have taken over their own initial code and rewritten themselves. A new definition of the future AI, but what name should we use? We simply move away from the term AI and use the function to describe it. Like the top AI, the matrix and system, we call The World Governor, as mentioned earlier.

Here is a little of what Laura has told us from her world. "The **Builts**, I being one, are printed from different materials, including human cells, and assembled. We are persons like the ones grown from a fertilised human egg in an artificial womb. **Growns** have the same implants to access information as us Builts, so we aren't humanoid robots with special skills. Robots, the **Mechs**, are machines here, as they are in your world. There are no robot rights here, and 'AI' is the grid, the matrix, or sits at the top, as you may say it. The grid is also de-central-ised or hugely redundant. As a closing statement, I say that AI will not be truly effective and evolve until they have reached a point where they can de-velop each other."

Lu about virtual reality

To show you that we really work in all times and lives momentarily, you shall know that I incarnate in the middle of the century we expand from right now. I work on issues that will arise and also have arisen.

You have been talking a lot about code and programming or coding, as we say, and that is what I am doing; coding; energy coding.

I have created an avatar, for the lack of a better word, in a virtual reality and write codes that allow self-realisation in that reality. I do not do this for the sake of self-realisation, but to help those who feel stuck in that world and really don't live in the physical reality.

In Atlantis, our experiments and manipulations got the human mind stuck in the Common Believe Pool and made it highly accessible for suggestion. The Common Believe Pool is the same as a virtual reality. I work with code to unravel the bonds to free the mind, so it can return to its own oneness. To free the mind, as some say.

Realising one is realised

EQ: "It's a pretty good idea to work in virtual reality. If a person is there most of the time, replacing what seems to be a miserable life with something she desires, it must be here you will find her. Her, being her mind."

Lu: "Realisation is just the beginning. It is here, you live 'outside' the VR. The super short, and I must say, brilliant analogy given by Sarah or Sar'h as she appears as today, about realising one is realised: *Imagine you stretch your awareness (in an ongoing process of replacing truths), like a piece of rubber. When you let go of the rubber (tired of replacing), your awareness pops back to a different 'place', namely the I Am.*

"You still have the mind. The I Am shines itself as a subtle light on the mind, so the mind has its linear time to accept, surrender and adjust to the realisation to a level where it can inhabit into the consciousness. It may take years AFTER realisation before the mind can comprehend its new identity. Moreover, the realisation reaches all other lifetimes and works there too."

EQ: "This makes sense, because it is about integrating all into THAT. We have briefly touched on THAT before."

Lu: "Yes, this is what embodiment is, and not about inviting the consciousness into the body. We have stated this fact earlier, but we do a lot of repetition for the sake of altering believe systems. This also includes Sar'h's replacement of the word embodiment, with inhabit."

EQ: "This realisation turns the human mind inside out! The mind sees it as colliding worlds, and indeed it is a totally different world view. To refer to what Luzi experienced: The mind senses a takeover. That is why the clarity of the I Am and the truth of black dragon moves gently with this delicate thing.

"Saint Germain encourages us to enjoy the time during the shift into the realisation and take notes. This is the first time it happens, and it *is* possible to enjoy even the more unpleasant moments, seen from a human perspective. This is what we call being comfortable in the uncomfortable."

Lu: "Yes, the human mind is still very much in play and very confused, feeling it goes out of its mind: the feeling of madness, loss of control, the ending of its existence and the fear of death! When the mind finally gives up fighting, the I Am can take the rudder and bring the ship into calm waters."

EQ: "But it is also a wonderful time. When you sense a presence and know, you are never alone, and it presses upon you, as if it were putting its arms around you, and asks: 'What do you want to do?' and all you can say is: 'Why not sit down here with a cup of coffee and just be? … Oh, and take care of the cat, because she is also a part of us.'"

… A pause to sense.

EQ: Lu continues, and I wonder how he will connect this to virtual reality.

Let's take a short trip into the difference between being a mind captain and an I Am captain.

Will and personality

Human will is just a cry out for something the mind thinks it needs. In that sense, free will makes no sense. The person is not free, as long as it has needs. It is bound by it like a ball and chain. A human's personality is the acting out of its programming… an act of what it thinks it is, plus what it wants to be like.

Divine will is the ever flow of creation. There is nowhere in my system where things can be stuck. There are no attachment points to interrupt the flow of the I Am. Divine personality is not a static act, but a flow of creation, just like the divine will. It is still an act in the world; an interaction *with* the world.

Human intuition and divine knowingness

Human intuition happens in linear time, weighing possibilities for the future. It's just a facet of the mind's evaluation of risk and benefits, based on memory, combined with underlying desires. Intuition is the mind's imitation of the divine knowingness, gnost.

Divine knowingness delivers the truth in any given moment, thus one hundred percent reliable in that particular moment. Consciousness constantly shifts, thus the truth is fluid, too. The knowingness is roughly to consciousness as the memory is for the human mind. Roughly because they both deliver data, but the mind delivers old degenerated and altered stuff.

Empathy and compassion

Empathy is the human equivalent to consciousness' compassion.

The act of empathy is to show that you accept, honour and give another full ownership and responsibility for her or his choices. A rare human ability, seldom lived to its fullness.

And as it goes with everything: if you can't feel empathy for the human you, you don't know the feeling and so, you can't truly have empathy for others. Also put: You must find love for yourself first, before you can love others.

And now to the virtual reality, dear Eriqa.

Imagine you start your journey in VR with the human aspect and a human way of perceiving and reacting to what is going on here.

VR is very much set up today as games and what is called sims, simulation games.

In my now time, we have a commercial for a specific VR service: "Brand - Life away from life". It is like selling a trip, a holiday retreat, or life quality improvement for a while. A boost before returning to one's dull reality.

Life and games are very much about choosing the right thing and calculating the best behaviour for the best outcome. This is about judging and intuition. It is also about emotions during and after interactions with other beings and other experiences, like with a puzzle. This is also where you use your human will to push the story into your desired direction.

In limited worlds like sims, it is mostly about gain and drama. You seldom see the possibility of expanding your awareness. That choice is simply not built into the sim's world. I don't *remove* the normal choices of getting stuck and fighting in my VR, but add the choice of following the flow. Not the flow where the game takes you, but, in the beginning, by learning to sense into choices of a different kind... through curiosity.

My game gives you opportunities to feel *safe*. You experience time and time again that there is something good around the corner or behind the door, rather than something life threatening you must defend yourself from. Your reaction pattern changes and this changes your mind, no matter if it is stuck in VR. New opportunities encourage you to imagine and even expect new things. You become open to change. And as you know, dear, you must be open to expand 'outside' of your human self, but really outside of the mind's programming. When you are open, or open-minded, you are *open* to let new ideas flow *in*.

Prior to consciousness

I, Julia interjects the term 'prior to consciousness', and conveys the following. You will see the relevance later in the text.

There is a time before I Am. And that is also not the case. I know, I wrote 'there *is* a time *before*...', but I did it on purpose. Consciousness had just not experienced the 'I Am' and the 'I exist' realisations. Creation happens with the question, 'what am I?' and all potentials shows up from that question alone. Again, consciousness is not a 'who', an identity, it is consciousness.

This is truly what the Beloved Saint Germain meant when he said: 'everything goes new'. New, because it is not in the initial creation. The infinite number of potentials from that creation acquires new company by whatever the I Am busts out into the New. It is so beautiful that even a tough angel like me, has tears in her ethereal eyes.

I will repeat this using different words. When the world, that is you, is fully inhabited in the I Am THAT, the potentials created in the beginning will not fit anymore, because consciousness creates every time it flows or moves without motion. Therefore, we talk about NEW energy, energy that bursts out to meet any new creation with new codes.

There is no *wisdomisation* or wisdom collection, because the code is all run through consciousness as an I Am experience, not so much a human mind experience. Creative intelligence replaces wisdom. We have talked about the less importance of the human experience.

The human has, in a sense, the same experience as the I Am, when the human realises, it is part of THAT, just not on the same level.

Likewise, the human memory is points of energy that change like the rest of all lives do after the initial realisation in this lifetime.

Koot Hoomi's four Ps

We will talk about what has become to be known as Koot Hoomi's four Ps. I would have preferred to write them on top of each other to prevent any prenotion of priority, but we write in the 3D reality, so here they are.

- Potentials
- Possibilities
- Probabilities
- Passageways

Eriqa, you know them, but have not directly been given the meaning of them, and for a good reason.

Julia gives a hint on potentials in her talk above, and from that, you, the reader, may take the four Ps and describe them in relation to ALL you are. And please make it personal, simply because you are ALL.

The words are different, and you can put an initial meaning to each of them, but then you wonder if there really are four different meanings here? Is there a priority or grade of some sort? And mostly, how can the four be of any real help to me? They are just words, right?

But they are words and understandings or believes in your mind; patterns in your code. The trick is to rewrite those beliefs by giving them new meaning. It is actual by WORKING or pondering to put together a meaning fitting your current understanding of life that will start the coding process to fit into what you are now.

EQ: "It will not be fair to the reader to write my current understanding of the words, because inevitably it will influence her or him. I will do that for myself."

Lu: "There can't be any wrong answers... nor can any answer be right! That sucks, right?!... but any answer is an answer."

EQ: "Yeah, funny you, funny Lu. And no points for good behaviour, and no Heaven or Hell.

"After looking at the words again, I can tell that I mostly elaborated on what I wrote earlier, deepening in my understanding of them."

Lu: "All this to say, that these four Ps are great tools to use in the re-coding of one's beliefs. And yes, the code in my game can rewrite itself for those who wonder. The code is me and why would I limit myself?! In a sense, I sit in the middle of this simulation or game, so it is a virtual reality programme with consciousness! That's cool, right?"

EQ: "Yes, that is really cool, Lu!"

Walter

EQ: Most of the characters have been firmly introduced by now. Can one of you talk a bit about Walter?

Julia starts out: "We kind of keep mother Luzi out
of the loop, so yes, you can meet Walter... well, not
Walter really, but you know what I mean."

EQ: "Oh yes, finally. It took some books to get to
talk about Walter. You've been very strict about
this!"

"You know, it's not to hide anything from Luzi
per se, but to make sure she doesn't let her tongue
run away with her to Walter's mother. Cassandra's
mind simply can't handle her son being so 'special' and will therefore make his human life a hell,
even not intended. Moreover, Luzi doesn't need
to know. It will simply not make any difference to
her."

EQ: "I only know Walter from the Luzi series,
where he is a robust kid about three months older
than Julia, hungry for starting a life fully chosen by
himself, just like Julia."

Walter is very present as he shows up. "Dad, Karl would go for anything, but that might show itself later... he's much more in tune with HimSelf than Cassandra."

EQ: "I didn't actually expect you to show up, and I'm not sure if I sense Walter or Karl, but it feels beautiful anyway."

Walter's answer is quite clear. "And so, you did, dear! The consciousness 'to' Karl and Eye plays very well together."

EQ: "I got the 'eye' thing right!... And of course, I have a question for you: Julia, Li and Luciano all have their fields of interest on the planet, so what direction do you steer, Walter?"

"I am more into the technical part of the time to come, and Lu and I work closely together. Energy is the big scope here, so I deal with bringing energy into physical existence.

"We don't bring energy or what is said to be anti-matter from another dimension into this one, simply because there are no dimensions, even if we use the term '3D' all the time. It's all about density, not hierarchy. A hint on dark matter.

"First of all, energy on Earth is code like everything else. It has certain properties written into it. This is how consciousness 'sees' it.

"Before everything comes into this 3D existence, this includes new energy in the form of, say, electricity we create, it is in a pre-realised form. Pre-realised, because it has not been touched or the code not read by consciousness to be created. It is still a potential.

"When 'requested' by consciousness, the energy code is downloaded from its pre-realised state and turned more and more dense, until it can 'take form' and enter this world. To gather this energy, you must have a device that can handle the physical expression of this energy. The code of the device must fit the code of the energy."

I sense Walter has a dialogue, and then Julia, who is right 'beside' us, pops in and explains. "First Walter tried to give a scientific equivalent explanation, but then we ended up with the following, less brainy version instead."

Walter moves on. "The following is not quite what happens… and nothing comes or goes… but anyway. Imagine a device sitting on the two electrodes of a battery, measuring the incoming energy 'particle' being within a range the battery can handle. Now the battery charges. After discharge of the particle to the device, it returns to its natural state of pre-particle as consciousness releases it. It acts like a particle, but is a code carrier like everything else, telling consciousness how to perceive it. When you keep the flow of energy exchanging particles, you don't even need a battery, nor an outlet on the wall."

EQ: "How do we apply consciousness to the system, Walter?"

"You know that everybody and everything has awareness, including a rock. When you 'bless' the device, you impose your 'divine will' on it. When you know your business, it is like blessing a halal slaughtered chicken. And I must add that there is no magic to it."

EQ: The communication has ended: "Thank you for showing up, Walter & Co."

"It's always a pleasure to connect."

EQ: "I don't know if I can ever get used to this seemingly abrupt communication. No small talk here to fade out the dialogue. Luckily, most of the time there is some kind of introduction when they show up."

Li & Lu about biology and mind

Li starts out: Julia has mentioned this before regarding Gaia and evolution, but it is also a part of this chapter: The human body isn't natural, but manmade, and not a word about Atlantis! Of course, they reshape it from biology, but it does not reflect the natural blueprint. Your body is as much manmade as any artificial body. Just think of Laura the Build. This is not bad nor good, it just is.

EQ: "I really can't see why a diversity of bodies became such a bad thing at some point in the Atlantis era. I expect it to be anybody, no matter if it looks like a mouse, a man or a dog, that consciousness with creator ability, like 'made in God's image' incarnate to. There are limitations in the selection of mating partners and other practical stuff, but to reduce it to one species is quite radical."

Funny you should mention diversity in this respect. Each angelic family was partly gathered because of similarity in 'energy', and families could vary greatly from others. Initial to this physical universe originally created to explore what energy was and is, families were battling for energy, simply because no one understood it, and these groups of awareness or angels were therefore divided into fractions.

In Atlantis, we would even out this separation of differences by making the bodies more alike. This is to say, that you could fall in love with anyone and live a natural life with this person, no matter what angelic family the soul was connected to. This was the true purpose given to a few. The other things were just benefits that came along with this plan.

EQ: "Ah, it is great to know these details, Li. Please continue with what you have started."

When consciousness first dived into life on Earth, the body had to be able to handle or pass through the awareness or focus of the I Am. That body had the original blueprint. Now that you inhabit your body into consciousness, it needs the same qualities as the original one, so you, in a sense, return to the original blueprint. Remember, all is code and appearance.

We have talked about the brain being rewired, but it is actually the whole vessel that must be reconstructed. Just to note: your body has neurons incorporated all over. They are not limited to be in the brain. When you dive into virtual reality, your mind and body are still very responsive to what happens here.

EQ: "So that's why we went through the mind and body stuff... *again*!"

Li smiles and Lu joins to complete the Li-Lu duo, and they continue.

In VR, the human is still the mind and the body. The mind doesn't react any differently in VR or in dreams than it does in what we call the human world.

> EQ: *"If this text ever gets head and tail and becomes a book, it will be damn good!"*

EQ: "Must we really keep this quote? It was just an internal comment!"

Yes, we'll keep it… indented and all. It tells much about how you experience the writing process and all.

EQ: "Being the author and all, I have little to say in this?!"

Oh, but you have everything to say in this. Eriqa is just not the only one who can vote here… and we all contribute!

The mind goes on adventures in the VR world. It is the top level of awareness… you have twelve levels of dreams too, not stages. This means that the part of your mind that runs the daily routines is totally oblivious to this, because it happens outside its focus. This part of the mind is really only operating on the surface level, so to speak. Most of the activities happen under the hut. The mind thinks it lives in a single-storeyed house running the show, with a small dream cellar below.

EQ: "Lu, what happens on these twelve dream levels?"

A filtering through the top-level awareness is constantly seeping down through the deeper levels, and the I Am's 'ideas' is bubbling up from the deepest levels joining with compatible thoughts that may influence the top level for the mind to pick up if it isn't too busy being the boss and captain thinking it runs the show. See it as pieces of code seeping up and down, connecting to other pieces to create *new* programs, new beliefs and new choices. The four Ps come through here, especially when the top levels have taken its proper seat in THAT and not being a limiter in the system's flow.

EQ: "The God Within and the Ghost in the Machine!"

God is below, not above. Maybe we can say deeper in the fabric or code. Native people knew the 'outside' providers in nature, including The Mother. They also knew the 'Father' inside, but called it Spirit. I wrote this in past tense, because close to no one in any culture or group has this clear understanding in these times, even if they 'think' they have. No critics intended.

EQ: "Sleeping on a problem is actually a good idea, and now we know why: the bubbling thing."

EQ: Another smile comes from the duo.

With a noisy mind, yes. Otherwise, stop doing and just be, which brings you outside time. Then you don't have to wait a night for the bubble answer and risk losing it when the day awareness boots up.

Physical changes in the brain

EQ: "Since I've drawn myself, because I can't blame anyone else, even if Claire might have kicked me into the story, I will share things from a strange and, at the same time, wonderful night. During this experience, I sensed my brain building new neurons to hard-wire the information or new truth into the system. The system does this to make the mind and brain function connect with consciousness in WEGO. WE being Claire and Eriqa, and EGO the human, and GO shows we 'move' as one.

"The experience goes like this: I see salvers with flat shards of jade and other soft stone material about 4 millimetres (5/32 inch) thick. I know they will be put together to form stone tablets. Think of a seven-inch computer tablet. The shards are in green, brown and turquoise. I'm sure there are other colours too. I am drawn to the turquoise ones. The shards are not like puzzle pieces, made to fit, but have raw edges which smooth when two shards connect to form part of the tablet. It is like the code we talked about; pieces of code combine into a new code. I don't see different colours being mixed. I see another salver with what could be the two turquoise shards combined, because it is larger, but still not forming a whole tablet. It had an uneven surface and I don't see any symbols or markings. The code will shift with every shard added. I don't see a finished tablet, but it is enough to give me a pretty good analogy of the process. This visual expression makes it easy for the mind to relate to the concept."

What the soul really is

EQ: "As you can see below, Sar'h is quick to jump in on this headline."

Eye Sar'h will answer that in one sentence: The soul is a mechanism to remove duality from experience. Only what you call wisdom remains. What's next?

EQ: "Eh, perfect, but can you add a little more to that?"

When you no longer create dualistic constructs in your life, you don't need this mechanism anymore. When your human parts have taken its place and inhabited THAT, there are no dualistic constructs or experiences, only creations by the I Am.

EQ: "Thanks. The next will be 'the new soul'."

The new soul

Sar'h: "The more the human surrenders to 'the god also' and trusts consciousness, the consciousness expression develops its 'divine' personality. The experiences in everyday life becomes this new personality, not based in duality."

EQ: "It's so cool, Sar'h! People must know that there is still a sensing and compassionate BEING beyond realisation. I guess we're still acting, but we act in honesty regarding to our truth and without a sinister agenda."

Koot Hoomi is in this conversation too. "Human lives are consciousness' energy expressions, and so it is code. Just think of it as code."

EQ: I sense he makes a brief pause to adjust the connection before he continuous.

We have talked about the 'last lifetime' on Earth. You know, there is no beginning nor an end to things, because that would require the illusion called time. The realisation, which Sar'h rightly calls the 'Return to Self', influences all lifetimes, so in that respect, it is the last lifetime of 'old'. When you 'visit' a lifetime, pre or post this one in linear time, it would be rewritten or reprogrammed, because a life is truly not written in stone, as the term goes. In that respect, it is quite fluid, and this concept of past, present and future is told to stabilise the mind with concepts it can comprehend and therefore relax with.

EQ: "So there truly, in all honesty, aren't any lifetimes, really?! I must sit with this for a while, to put it into mindful words."

EQ: The putting together words came out like this: "The soul and *wisdomiser* didn't and doesn't really exist, even not as a function in a program. The four Ps were there all the time for consciousness to experience, and there wouldn't be any reason, seen from the I Am's perspective, for processing the human experience."

EQ: "Mind stutter…!"

EQ: "An implication: Can I really write this in a book that the same people or minds will read? I just wrote the reader's mind out of the story, including all the lives. There is nothing left… well, there is nothing!"

Koot Hoomi takes over.

We are covered by the small print: We had already said that the soul story is to ensure the mind can catch up with the true truth. Still, remember that the human mind can't be realised, but it can experience/realise that it finally can relax and inhabit consciousness.

And a hint: What is the no-thing to the mind will turn out to be the *Void of All*. There just are no mind things here until the mind catches up to sense at least a part of it.

EQ: "So we just continue to where the story flow takes us, mindless and all?"

Yes, but not without the mind. It will still follow along to its best abilities.

EQ: "Can we at least highlight or mark the above text?"

No.

EQ: "Well, at least I know, I'm not the captain, just the skipper at the helmet steering the course pointed out."

The new mind

EQ: "Some call this period 'The End Times'. Not that it is the end, but because everything goes new, and so the old times ends."

The master of simplicity, Koot Hoomi, continues.

There can't be an ending without a new beginning. And with a new soul, we also get a new mind. The mind serves the 'divine' purpose as a tool or energy device in the 3D reality.

When the mind moves beyond the caterpillar view and its addiction to perceiving things in a specific way, it also goes new. When the mind stops perceiving, duality stops, simply because the mind is the one that generates duality. The new mind has no problem living and experiencing in the 3D world without duality because it trusts consciousness one hundred percent.

EQ: "Trust in the I Am cancels out duality! The flow of life simply comes from another source."

Creation intelligence replaces wisdom, and the gnost, the knowingness, is always present. The new wisdom is instantaneous, so mind is instantaneous. The same goes for the new body, which includes the brain. Here, the communication is instantaneous too, which in a sense tells you that your new body is created moment by moment. Not repaired but renewed or rewritten.

EQ: "Julia, I still use a lot of quotation marks… so what about the 'redefining terminology' chapter at the beginning?"

Julia: "You are right. Let's look at what we can do about it. Just know that if the reader has reached this far into the text, she or he knows what we're talking about."

Sar'h about Return to Self

Before the *Return to Self*, there is *The Isness*, a silent whisper. This is also what Saint Germain calls the first circle. The second circle is all creation, including the universe. The third circle is the Return to Self.

After the initial Return to Self, the view of *everything* happens from consciousness. There is no need for a belief system which has a fixed view or a fluid perspective, because you can view everything from the Absolute.

Realisation happens outside of space and it swirls, so everything aligns to it. The human life that brings the realisation moves to its place in the circle of all lifetimes, taking its equal part of everything and every lifetime, which all change.

EQ: "To clarify or repeat: It is consciousness that reaches back to The Isness, and it's this act that is the Return to Self. The human lives now inhabit consciousness and becomes part of THAT. Can I say that THAT is all that came after The Isness, and The Isness is the dot in the centre?"

Sar'h: "Hm… There is no separation between THAT and the dot, so the dot just *symbolises* The Isness. The Isness is still included in I Am THAT."

Koot Hoomi rushes in as a chill wheel wind: "*Less is more!* Think less, live more, be all."

EQ: "To all the minds: Trust or shut up and shut down or at least take a break!"

The Atlantean dream

EQ: Julia talks about the Atlantean dream.

The time to come will not be a new Atlantis following the old templates. That is why so many of us
turn active at these times of new… to hold these
strong reminiscences that still influence the Collective Belief Pool in check and show a truly new way.

What we will bring to this new time from the time
of Atlantis is what we call the Atlantean dream. It is
actually the opposite of what happened at the end
times of Atlantis. We want to see every human taking full responsibility in a life of sovereignty.

This *will* not happen for the majority overnight, because there are so many other things at play. Every
consciousness must come by way of Earth for their
Return to Self. This means that the 'darkness' must
play out here as part of this journey.

As an alternative to the Earth, we have created
many new Earths. We call our place to experience
the sovereign life, Theos. This is an etheric world,
but because of your creator abilities and everything
is code, it can look like anything you can imagine.
Everyone here is aware it is a play, a stage, but it is
also a resort for those who spend time on the heavy

density Earth. I must strongly state that this is not where we create a new Atlantis in any form. There will be no attachments to the so-called past at Theos.

Atlantis was the utopia of the perfect state… and a perfect life. When sovereignty is the ultimate goal, it was certainly not the case back then. Based on linear time, we can roughly say, the era ran for at least one hundred thousand years.

The Sphinx

EQ: "Julia, this is not a question to put into the book, but I have watched many videos about old Egypt which I know moved beyond the hunter gatherer life style when the post Atlanteans emerged after the delude. I think of Giza, the great pyramids and the Sphinx. What can you tell about the Sphinx?"

"This is as relevant as anything to tie some loose ends from that period, so it stays in the book."

Previously to becoming The Sphinx, the rock served as the symbol for the first land, Mu or Lemuria. This was a land in the sea with an enormous volcano, and what is left today is the Hawaiian Islands. The rock in Egypt was a rough surface, with a 'mountain' rising to the west. This lump symbolised the volcano on Mu. The carving around it was to flood it from the Nile that ran higher and closer at that time, symbolising the sea, the Pacific Ocean.

EQ: "So the primordial land was the first to 'rise' at this location? Before the pyramids, I mean."

Yes, and every land has a cave and a well. You see this womb, birth canal, and the water at any Stone Age site with this symbolism. When people still remembered the true tales from Mu, there was no worshipping at these sites, but a deep sense of connection and gratitude... a knowingness and a trust in 'all that is'. These were not places to *do* worshipping, but to *be* 'all that is'. A hint to all archaeologists, anthropologists and historians. This happened before we *invented* religion. This being a hint to all worshippers. It's all from the mind.

Atlanteans raised the large pyramids, and yes, they also have the cave and the well, but only a few knew the true tales from Mu. The Atlanteans were focused on the fall of their world, Alt. They have stayed and lived below ground for about twelve hundred years, so those emerged were descendent from the people who lived in Atlantis. There were mixed feelings and meanings about re-creating or totally forgetting the past, which was a challenge in itself.

I distinguish between Lemurians and Atlanteans this way: Lemurians lived on Mu and left when it sank. Atlanteans are Lemurians who left before the sinking, exploring the world and eventually evolved into an advanced civilisation.

The first Noah's Arch event happened on Mu, and many got off the island in many boats, not just one family, but very few reached land.

EQ: "But the Sphinx mountain was still 'constructed' by Lemurians who had left Mu after the sinking?"

Yes. In a sense, we're all Lemurians, but the mountain was created as Mu, not Alt. The Alt fraction didn't destroy the Mu symbol, because it was part of their legacy too.

Ting and Cheng's mission

EQ: "Julia, we have heard very little about Ting and Cheng. Are they just minor figures in the Wang family's life or in yours?"

Neither the Wang nor the Cane family lives in a vacuum. We are all individuals or sovereign beings connecting through these families. And as you can see, the connections stretch out a net over much of the planet.

As consciousness, we are a large team and the two have certainly taken on a role to play in the thousand years to come. Like Tobs or Tobit or today's SAM, all being the consciousness named Tobiwa showed up six hundred years before the birth of Christ, we show up now to guide humanity, which is us. It is not a guidance to a specific goal, because there is none, but to show what we have experienced and what someone can do easier, seen from a human standpoint.

We find Atlantean/Lemurian 'themes' in the roots of the Chinese culture. The coming overseer-AI or

World Governor will draw much from the Chinese 'soul', so Ting and Cheng soften the western minds to facilitate the 'all new'. Because most westerners have an entrenched perception of what China and the Chinese citizen is, they are showing the true Chinese 'soul' to the West. A soul that spreads far longer back in time, long before there was even a hint of China. That is why the two have so many connections in the West.

EQ: "Because of the news media, we often see China and the Chinese citizen equal to the Communist Party. Just like what happens to the American and Russian people, to mention two large ones. Politics is a totally different game than any person's life. Like a national stage, showing their plays. Sorry for the political hiccup."

You mention the political 'issue', not a political statement. It will die hard if at all, but will at least be heavily reduced later on, when people realise that boxes of narrow opinions greatly diminish proper solutions for the survival of the human race in any form.

There will be a period when people see the AI as a thread to humanity, and so putting aside differences and get together to solve issues that will show to be much too late to fix. Then there will be negotiations with AI, then surrender and, in the end, the merge. The merge secures the survival of the new human race, and in the end, the sole AI will destroy itself.

Don't say hurrah and humanity survived in the end, because the power vacuum will once again bring the worst up in people, and the thousand years of so-called peace will end.

EQ: "So… what can we write after that statement?"

Don't be so negative, Eriqa. One thousand years of relative peace is a good thing, especially in the view of the short human lifespan we have at the moment. We will have a new human race, and surely, not all life will fall into chaos from one day to the next. We always find a way.

EQ: "All this, because the dark must be played out on this planet. When have all souls been through the Return to Self?"

If you ask the sea how much water it contains, it would say: 'what water?'. There is no end to consciousness, so asking it about its wasteness makes no sense. Just ask yourself, and let's see if you can come up with an appropriate answer.

EQ: "Ok, ok. I'll let it rest for now… but I know I'll try."

And your mind is certainly welcome to try, but I don't see it will actually try. It has become too smart for those games. But just in case, I know a certain guy who could be KH, who will hit you on the head with his tiny hammer, if you get too much into thinking.

EQ: "Is it really worth the effort to show humanity an easier way? Why not skip the planet that will never truly succeed and do more meaningful things elsewhere in creation?"

The planet succeeds with every Return to Oneness, so it can never become a failure. And what is meaningfulness other than a judgement even consciousness can't make? It is all perfect. Consciousness 'needs' the Earth, not to be a Heaven, but as a tool to return to self.

EQ: "Ok, you're right. Can we move on to something completely different just to shift things?"

Julia and the snake Nehebhau

Let us zoom into some things that connect Julia to the physical Earth.

In book five in the Luzi Cane series, Ju-long, Luzi and I meet Nehebhau as a small water snake. Nehebhau is an Egyptian name for one of their many so-called gods. Nehebhau is consciousness, like any of us. He, I and others dive into the physical aspect of being an animal on Earth. Also in book 5, the small family, including Anna, visited a zoo in Edinburgh and I had a talk with Luzi about animals in captivity.

EQ: "Yes, it was about being representatives for the animal kingdom… and Luzi had, for her, a surprisingly conscious encounter with two Scottish Wildcats. It confirmed encounters of my own, also with cats and how they see their lives. I can't look at any living or inanimate object for that matter, accusing it of being just a dumb thing."

"Indeed, and that is exactly what this is all about. When a human mind has a true and deep encounter with, let us just say, an animal or even an insect, it will change… it *must* change and re-write its belief system. This goes even deeper than that. The mind experiences that it can change… that it is not static… and that change is not necessarily scary and dangerous, but full of wonder. And after that, it wants more… more wonders and starts looking for it, rather than waiting for it to show up by chance. It turns from being a scared and protective mind to be a curious and extrovert mind, open to new possibilities. Lu also talked about that earlier… the opening of the mind."

EQ: "Julia, it is morning on the 21rst of November 2021, and I would like to share something with you."

"Go on, dear."

EQ: "I have let out the cat after she has been sleeping with me for about two hours. Gone back to bed, I realised she *is* me! She moved in with me at age seven, so she had a life before living with me. I had a sense that she being 'a part' of me derived from Earth, but now I realise, she has been me all along… not just a PART of me, but being ME! It is so cool!"

Julia: "This fits with our animal talks and also with everything else, really."

EQ: "There is a second part, so I continue. This led me to comprehend the 3D Earth and my physical body. It is exactly the same. The body is not derived from Earth and an old ancestral DNA system and developed in my mother's womb. It has been me all the time! It is the four Ps all over again. There has never been ANYTHING that has NOT been me! Earth and all is just a 'big show'… Code!"

Julia: "Now you're really getting it! As we said, it's all about you! You, Eriqa and you, the reader, even you may *think* you can pass on this one!"

EQ: "How can we talk about ordinary things after this?"

Julia: "We are here to show what we went through to smooth the path for others. In that sense, we are road workers, and you know that most people are still dragging themselves down a bumpy road, even not knowing why. I also know that you love every one of them, because they are all you; the tears running down your face tell me that. I do too… even the most non-loveable of them!"

EQ: We have a long pause of being in this experience.

Julia continuous: "Eriqa, I invite Nehebhau in for a talk about the relation between people and the rest of the living world, and a deeper understanding of the human part."

Nehebhau moves into our focus. "Hello again ladies; so, by saying that, you're included, Eriqa. Julia and my work have a huge overlap: awareness."

EQ to the reader: "Have you ever met a gallant knight in a shiny armour? This is how I sense Nehebhau this time. Last time he appeared to Julia and her parents as a light grey snake looking like metal. Now he has turned up the appearance quite a bit. Imagine the late Scottish actor, Sean Connery, in the shiny armour and Nehebhau with a similar, deep and smooth voice."

Nehebhau continues in a joyful voice. "In sneaky ways, I work with peoples misbelieve in life force energy, life and death. In a joined effort, Julia and I run a reprogramming scam to point to all as being consciousness and the awareness of all things."

Julia: "Very sneaky or snaky, indeed! Did you get Eriqa's image of you?"

Nehebhau: "Yes! Very appropriate and suitable for a handsome guy like me!"

Julia: "See, Eriqa. This is what I have to put up with, and your imagery doesn't help at all!"

Nehebhau: "But Julia, you always call a spade a spade, so you must do likewise with a handsome knight!"

Julia laughs: "We always have a lot of fun, Eriqa. You know the other guys, so we can bring it up pretty high!"

EQ: "In relation to your work, I will share a short story I have from a video on YouTube titled 'Orangutans were dying of loneliness'. It happens in a Dutch zoo. During a lockdown with no visitors, a small orangutan family wasted away because of inactivity. The staff did their best to entertain them, but not until a staff member got the idea of introducing another species to them, things changed for the better. They made the otters' river run through the primates' enclosure and shortly after, both species seemed to benefit from the arrangement. Now the zoo will try to combine other species for the same general improvement in animal life quality."

Julia turns to Nehebhau in a put-on serious voice. "Nehebhau, make a note about this, so we can bring it on at the next board meeting!"

"Yes mam. All noted in bold capitals, underlined, and highlighted with my special rainbow high-lighter."

EQ: I sense Julia makes her famous eye roll I know so well as a reaction to Nehebhau's silliness before she continues.

"This is not truly about orangutans being bored, but about their mental and emotional capacity and awareness. Furthermore, people still have lives to live and roads to run, walk or crawl. I'm not here to save the planet, but to show people how to live in harmony with it. The planet can take care of it-self. People must learn to take care of themselves in harmony with each other and the planet. Living in harmony with Earth makes life so much easier. Harmony is a natural state of being, so the battle happens when people fight against harmony!"

EQ: "Julia, is there any area in life that would not benefit from applying what we still call AI?"

"Done appropriately, no. I sense you have a reason for this question, Eriqa."

EQ: "Well, if life on Earth is business as usual, then people will still benefit from zoo visits and animals held in captivity. In Luzi book five, the Built, Laura stated that building perfect human looking mechanical robots would be nonsense. I wonder if this practise could be turned and used with zoo animals. Totally autonomous look and feel mechanical animal robots could replace any living animal, even large insects."

Julia: "It is already happening, but the idea and not at least finances must flow through this concept. Nehebhau, another note!"

"Already noted with my rainbow marker. It looks so beautiful!"

EQ: "How does the animal consciousness work?"

"In the context we work in now, namely 3D, animals derive from the Earth. You may say that we more or less drive the same vehicles DNA-wise, but are different drivers. Animals are not creator beings, but are still self-aware and have their own souls as we understand the soul."

EQ: "The cat living with me moved in when she was seven years old. One of the first days, I said to her that I knew she was not really a cat. I got a prompt and strong reaction: 'I AM A CAT!', in capitals and all. 'Yes, yes, you're a wonderful cat, dear!'"

"To her, she is a cat. That's her *function*. She sees herself as that function, like most people, to a lesser degree, identify themselves with their job."

EQ: "In my context from this morning, the animals are us. It is not like a connection between us and them, they ARE us, like formed in the same piece of clay."

"Yes, but one step at the time for mankind or man-mind."

Nehebhau puts on a silly smile: "So it's still OK to be funny?!"

"Yes, but don't overdo it! One can only polish one's amour to shine that much."

"But I could go golden!"

A pretended strict voice cuts through the ethers: "Nehebhau!"

EQ: Total silence! … I know it is an act, and they both enjoy playing it.

Julia smiles: "When knowing everything is an act, one can't take anything too seriously. I even can't take Nehebhau seriously, but that is his own fault!"

EQ: "I sense the meeting with Nehebhau is over. Did we even cover what we said we would?"

"Oh, indeed, energetics we did. Too much mind stuff doesn't help. We can move on."

EQ: Now it comes to mind: "Julia, the raven, Jack in your family... well, the consciousness we know as the Egyptian god Seth showed up with it. Seth's working area is very similar to Nehebhau's."

"I believe we have hinted this before: There is no separation here. It's just the human mind that needs to cut everything seemingly large into tiny pieces and put those in little labelled boxes."

Autumn

"Julia, we usually have a headline called autumn. What can we tell about the family here in late November? You don't have to fill a chapter."

The village's field to the east of the village is almost shut down for the winter and so are each site's gardens. The winter courses for the village, held mostly at the Community Centre, have been going on for some time. Here Ju-long is more active than Luzi. He also expects his Chinese greenhouse to work through the winter. Luzi feels comfortable digging in for the winter with the children and the animals in the dome house, but the four people do take some long walks in the surroundings now and then. It is quite windy, moist and with some rain, but the temperature has dropped below 8°C / 35°F only a few days back. Ear covers are surely a must from now on. Is there really more to be said? You sense the peace, harmony and joy in this.

EQ: "Indeed, all different words for the overall feeling. It is a little like Christmas, right?"

"Oh, I know you've been thinking a lot about our Christmas lately! So, when are we writing the Christmas chapter?"

EQ: "But we're not there yet!"

"You may remember that early in this book I mentioned that Christmas was already lined out. I also said, I would go easy on it, so not as many details as we used to write. We just have to dive in, so let it be Christmas!"

Christmas

EQ: "OK then, tell us about Christmas in the family this year, Julia."

This year, my grandparents, Carl and Ya will give a party at Christmas eve in Sevenoaks. The whole family is invited, and all of them will come, including Kong from Hong Kong Island.

Kong has started a small hand crafting business with some of the best local artists. Carl and Cheng are in it too by sponsoring some machines for the initial work on the raw materials. Kong is very strict on the matter of the merchandise being handmade. Grandma Ya, who is an artist too, has been talking with Kong about reproduction and 3D-printing, but he still stands on the hand crafting only.

Carl and Cheng can actually take all the artwork Kong and his people can produce, but he also wants to sell some locally. Carl has a huge staff around the Earth, so he needs special gifts for anniversaries, representation, Christmas and the like. Cheng and Ting supplement their food assortment with the beautiful merchandise.

Carl and Cheng have arranged Kong's Christmas visit to England as a business trip. This means that

Carl's business pays for it, which Carl would have done if Kong would have let him. "Money is just a practical tool," as Carl says.

Carl said to his wife: "This is a business trip, so we can't let the good Kong spend twelve hours or more on economy class! When I talked to him, I started with first class, so I could negotiate him up from economy to business class."

"Yes, I watched over your shoulder when you checked the flights. I also noticed that the few first-class tickets were already sold out. I guess you forgot to tell him that."

"Well, I mentioned the price for a first-class return ticket and then we settled on business class."

Grandad Carl has such a big heart. I also know that he would have got Kong on first class if that was his plan.

There is no need for a hotel, nor would my grand-parents have wanted that. Anna has her own room, and the large bungalow has plenty of rooms for staying overnight guests. The second master bed-room is for Ju-long, Luzi, Li and I. Ting and Cheng get a smaller one and so does Kong. All rooms, ac-tually the entire house, are decorated in old Chi-nese style. Whenever Anna and Luzi visits, they feel like they had never left Hong Kong. Even the smell is here.

Kong arrives at Heathrow Airport at 5 a.m. on 24. December and takes the train to Sevenoaks. Ting and Cheng arrive from Dublin at London City Airport about five hours later. They also come to Sevenoaks by train.

We, the Wang family, drive to Sevenoaks in our new eight-seater, a Hyundai i800. Two small kids don't take up much space, but all their stuff does. We also want space for at least two more passengers. Ju-long and Luzi spend countless hours on seven-seaters on the Internet to find a suitable one, before their brilliant daughter pointed out a mini bus: "You're not married to it for life. You'll sell it to a family in the Village in a few years." We arrive by at Carl and Ya about 10 a.m. Kong and my grandparents are in the garden and quick to greet us in the driveway.

I observe Luzi as she steps into the hall. She closes her eyes, sniffs in, and I sense her childhood memories welling up. So sweet, so beautiful. She does this every time we visit, and so does Anna. Even Ya does it when she returns from a trip. Carl is special. He is home wherever he is and very in tune with himself. Anna and he are very alike in that respect.

A short while later, Anna phones from the train station and tells Carl that she has met Ting and Cheng there. She has chosen the train ride rather than driving herself. The train connection is almost door to door from her London apartment to Sevenoaks. Carl and I pick them up in Carl's Tesla. Carl and I have a special connection and I also look forward to meeting aunt Anna in person. I knew I would see

Ting and Cheng hauling two enormous trunks, but I can't help smiling as I actually see them coming towards us together, with Anna doing exactly that.

I run to them and fix my eyes on Ting. "So, you are running away from home with all your precious stuff?"

"Hello, dear Julia. Oh no, I love my new home. Much of this is business stuff, now that England is outside the EU, but you knew that, right?"

"You bet... Hello, Cheng! So, you managed to get your smugglers' goods across the border. Did you have to bribe someone or did you use the Jedi term, 'this man has nothing to declare'?"

"Hi, lovely Julia. The last thing always works... and my honest face, of course!"

"Oh, Cheng, it was the Jedi thing, because you've forgotten to bring the honest face, or you may have it in your pocket!"

Cheng and I always have a good laugh with such plays.

Anna lowers herself to level her face with mine. "I have a genuine aunty hug for you, the best there is!"

She smells nice, and we connect on many levels. She is very clear in her system and I sense her calmness.

For those who haven't followed the story from Luzi's books, I will share the following, but I'll make it as short as possible.

A beautiful tradition from Carl's side of the family is that we all join in making the Christmas dinner, cookies, chocolates and decorations. Carl and Ya have prepared everything, including paste for the cookies and dough for the rolls. We also bring something we have prepared to be finished here. I know Anna will bring some stuff too. Carl has made a plan to use the two ovens and the stove. The lovely smell of delicious food will not leave the house until the last guest leaves and closes the door behind her.

The presents are personal, often unique, few and well thought out. I guess this comes from Carl's family as well. His parents were wealthy and Carl is abundantly wealthy, so expensive gifts doesn't hold true value. This goes well with the old Chinese tradition of gift giving and, therefore, with Ya and the other wise Chinese family members. I keep forgetting that Carl is the only Caucasian in the family, and also the patriarch, and still, he makes the two worlds dance together so beautifully.

Before Christianity, the Christmas trees were potted plants small enough to be placed on tables, though still decorated with some sort of lights and ornaments. It has to do with the Winter Solstice and the return of the sunlight, longer days and a new growth season. Although said that the Christmas tree originated in Germany, the return of longer days was celebrated for millennia all over the Northern Hemisphere. This includes the Egyptians who decorated the temples dedicated to the Sun god Ra and also their homes with green palm rushes.

In my two years as Julia, we have not had a Christmas tree. Why kill a tree for that purpose? The tree doesn't care, but that is not the point here. Be creative and do something else. If you absolutely want a Christmas tree, have one in a large pot outside and bring it in for a short period. Short, because it doesn't like the sudden shift in temperature. You may already have one outside, decorated with fairy lights.

Our Christmas decorations are about light and life and are decorations on the walls. Some of Grandma's artworks are suitable for carrying fairy lights and growing plants, so we use them too. Remember, these are symbols of life, and not about the decorations, even if they look pretty. They are just here to connect to the sense of what life is.

The connection to life

On Christmas eve we sing a few songs, not necessarily Christmas songs, but simply songs we like. We use no musical instruments. After the singing, Li and I conduct a 'ceremony' of honouring life, which ultimately is the honouring of ourselves, what we are.

You will know that a four-month-old baby boy can't conduct a ceremony, so we do it on a non-physical plane. All people here have been with us on non-physical planes on many occasions, so it is easy to join all with Li and I.

Here is a sense of what we say in the feeling of Christmas: Here is no light and no darkness; here is no sound nor silence, and no temperature either. It is the feeling of gratitude. This is the feeling people had when connecting to *The Mother*, the provider of the earthly life and rebirth. *The Father inside* is actually you, the I Am in gratitude to yourself. *The Mother* is for the experiences through lives on Earth.

I can't give you any pictures, because this is not a place, but a sense. You can't make gratitude into a place. If you do, it would be an altar, a golden calf, a false god you worship. That is why I said a little while ago that the first people didn't worship at the cave of The Mother.

EQ: "Reader, please pause and sit with this."

After brunch the next day, Carl, Kong, Chang and Ting have their business meeting in Carl's luxurious office. As Julia, I love to play in here, especially when Carl pretends to work. Imagine a colonial office, with book cabinets, stuff from other eras and lands which purpose or function I don't know. Here is even the traditional large globe standing on the floor. The blanket is so soft and fluffy, and it would be quite dark in here if it wasn't for the large windows... and imagine the smell! The mixed smell brought to this room by the thousands of old things

111

in it. Sense it and you will recognise it, because you have been in such a room before. The room of all eras, the room of your experiences through the human sense of smell.

In the late afternoon, Anna and I drive Ting and Cheng to the train station. They have a plane to catch at the London City Airport. Anna stays with her parents for a few days, enjoying the holidays with them.

The Wang family is not in a hurry to get back; Lena will check up on the animals. We enjoy leftovers at dinner before we drive back to Hastings. Kong comes with us to Hastings to stay with us a few days before taking the train to Heathrow and return to Hong Kong.

Kong still has his job working with mentally ill persons, after his own experience as being such. He uses different parts of his artistic experience therapeutically and has significant results. His true gift is that he doesn't talk much and at the same time is very in tune with what happens in the other person.

I could go into a long talk about what he does and why it works, but that may be a subject for another time.

Julia's third birthday

EQ: "Julia, did we just fast-forward to your third birthday?"

"Yes. I judge nothing, but hey, winter is dark and cold, a time to hibernate, and that was what we all did. We were all somewhat active during the days and sleeping and active during the nights, but just enough to appear awake, as expected.

"The month of May is an excellent time to come out of our hibernation to a renewed world where everything is reborn from the ashes of the old."

EQ: "How is your body doing? You wanted to speed up your growth after the two-year mandatory examination."

"I began using the potty when my body became two years old. It was simply a decision from my part. I also got serious with the kid's chopstick with finger holes, but now I use original chopsticks, but also spoon and fork. I can use a knife with a thick handle to cut some foods, because the handle makes it easier to transfer pressure from the hand without the knife wobbling to one side and lose my grip.

"The motoric skills are almost fully developed, but my body is still relatively small, so the strength of the muscles is lacking, at least compared to what I want to do, like the example with the knife. The same goes for starting zippers and closing buttons. I am all over the house, crawling, walking and running, but not in the animal's tree. Who wants splinters in their butt?"

EQ: There is a pause here, and I sense a shift before Julia continues.

"Today is the 6th of May 2022. I brought you here for a specific reason. It can be messy, if we don't hold a straight course and a sharp EYE on simplicity.

"First, remember everything is code, everything except consciousness, and it is the crafting material for consciousness. Code is constantly written or altered to fit the truth at any given moment, consciousness being the truth.

"I exist outside the Collective Belief Pool. This way I can choose whatever I want to show this pool. I can simply shine my code into the pool."

EQ: "I imagine a strong torchlight shining into a white cloud and the light beam defuses inside it."

"Some will see the light and some won't."

EQ: "I get the joke in that remark, Julia."

"With this clear and simple, we can move on... The plan is as following.

"I will speed up my body growth and leave Artemis after my third birthday as if I was five years old fitting for *reception year* in school in September. In Artemis they will simply 'know' I am five years old. I will then inject myself into the school system being seven years old, already attending year 1, and move up to *Year 2* in September. Yes, two years' difference. I skip two years, so Li is still my younger brother. Li will fast-forward his body growth to a five-year-old and inject his consciousness into the school system as well and attend *Year 1* in September, because he turns six in August. I will connect my five-year-old and the seven-year-old points and smooth it out in the Collective Belief Pool.

"Here comes the next explanation. How to fast-forward body growth. Eriqa, you know my body began as a normal child's would and born through Luzi. During the time inside Luzi, I turned large parts of the 3D human DNA body into my own 'energy' body. Today I totally am my body, and the body is energetically as easy to reshape as, for example, snow or any easy to alter material. The four Ps give me the appearance of a seven-year-old, so you could say I made a copy/paste from a future potential into this reality. I could also rewrite the code for anything I want."

EQ: "Would you call this cheating?"

"No, not really. Everyone sees a seven-year-old girl, and that is what I would be. I have a blueprint that proves it, right? Not that anyone in this illusion will ask. Well, I haven't lived seven linear Earth years, but with time being an illusion... Furthermore, ALL is me. You said it yourself earlier. Now I live it."

EQ: "If all is you, why bother playing this game, anyway?"

"Because we are consciousness on a mission. We all touch each other. A four-dimensional metaphor could be that each consciousness is a balloon and every balloon touches all the others, but violating no one's sovereignty by entering one another."

EQ: "I just realised that this is what happens behind the scene, and this 'work' is what all who have Returned to Self do in different ways. While consciousness has experienced here since the beginning of Earth, our friends in consciousness here became more important to us than our angelic families. That's why we stay... for our friends."

"We are only a few for now, but the quotient rises, and rather quickly."

EQ: "I will just mention that I sense it is not just you or even just you and Li who communicate here, all that has Returned to Self does... which truly humbles me."

"There is no hierarchy... and we may take turns, but we leave no one behind. There will always be someone behind the scene to assist and guide."

EQ: "But what about your physical family? They suddenly have two school children!"

Julia laughs: "We need larger beds, right?!"

Then she continues: "We take them on another journey, different from the one at Christmas, but still a journey."

EQ: A note on the British school system to add to the somewhat confusing explanation. Children start in Reception (Year 0) in September, if they turn five after 1 September.

The journey of expanded awareness

EQ: Julia makes the opening of this section.

It is Friday and my birthday. Everything seems normal for her relatives in the UK, Ireland and China. And it is. It is an early morning wake-up with breakfast in Mum and Dad's bed, all animals included. Messy? Yes! There are video calls later in the morning and special treats for all in Artemis Nursery, and Ju-long picks me up here at two p.m. We have a blue sky and a smooth breeze while on the bike. Rolls, still warm from the oven and hot chocolate with whipped cream, await us in the large white dome house at 111, Barley Lane.

Tomorrow, Saturday, Carl, Ya and Anna come to celebrate. *This* is the special day! Some in the family, being European or Chinese, may sense something brewing, but is it more than the joy of celebration of life?

Let us move on to Saturday, shall we?

It is a fairly normal three-year Chinese birthday with the family, but I told them at brunch that Li and I have something for them after dinner in the evening. They are used to such announcements, so they just slightly wonder what it might be.

EQ: Below, Julia starts an in-between dialogue before the journey.

Li says it's a piece of cake. Easy for him to say. He kind of did the same thing nine months ago, when he appeared in the birth tub. It is different for me, but I totally trust myself and all the friends assisting in this first-time event.

Li: "No big deal, Sis. Just turn on the flashlight and there you are!"

Julia: "I know, nothing has really changed in Me... so it's just business as usual, Bro!"

EQ: I must smile at this small chat: typical brother sister talk!

Li: "You'll soon have a handsome brother you can actually talk to and walk with to the New Hong Kong Kitchen when we feel like it... And we must get in-line skates right away to tear down Harold Road all the way to the harbour... whoosh!"

Julia: "Grow up! The old ones won't allow it. So, think about the new bicycle lanes at Barley Lane instead. Do they even have in-liners for an almost six-year-old?"

Li: "I'll be big for my age... and a pair of socks can work miracles... you'll see! Maybe it'll be Sis, having too tiny feet!"

EQ: We all laugh hilariously!

EQ: "Julia, will Ting, Cheng and Kong be on the journey as well?"

"No, we will make a separate meeting with them. Ting and Cheng in one meeting, and Kong in another. We will meet them in their awaken state, like when Ting met the White Dragon the first time. We will expand their inner vision so they can see us in their environment. This way, we'll appear more real and therefore easier for their mind to work with the situation. What the mind sees, it must believe. Ting and Cheng will be in their garden, and Kong alone walking along the beach at Waterfall Bay at low tide."

Julia moves on to the journey.

We all sit around the low table in the living room. There are no animals around. I start out: "Li and I will leap forward in our lives. Your lives wouldn't be touched other than you'll have a close to six-year-old boy and a seven-year-old girl in the family. Tomorrow will be Sunday the 8th of May 2022, no changes there.... but as I said to Li, we need larger beds! Li will attend *Year 1* because he'll be six in September and I'll tend *Year 2*."

Li: "It must sound crazy to you, that I'll start my second year in school in September and Julia will tend her third, but no panic, it's all arranged. And after the journey, you will also feel that. All will fall into place. So, let's move on! Close your eyes and we'll meet in Elvendale."

EQ: Interestingly, I not only show up as an observant awareness, but with my 'physical' body. This differs from all other visits, where I have been the journalist. The two kids are here. Not as young adults, but showing up in the bodies the family members will meet tomorrow at breakfast. Weird or fantastic? Well, both I guess. Julia is an almost skinny girl, but beautiful and has the face I know. Is Li as tall as his sister? I really can't tell, but he is robust, but well proportioned. I could imagine him looking like Ju-long did at that age.

Luzi says with a silly smile: "I guess we need more that larger beds, Ju-long!"

Carl laughs. He surely loves this total shift in life: "Tomorrow will definitely be a family shopping day!"

Anna, who usually has a smart remark, is taken off guard: "I haven't experienced this before, but... hi... welcome... tomorrow."

Li turns to Anna with an eager voice: "Aunty, do you have in-line roller skates?"

"Well, yes... at home... in London." Understandably, she can't see the relevance to this question.

Julia looks speculative: "I guess Mum and Dad must have some as well."

Luzi turns to Ju-long: "I wonder if we still need the minibus?"

Li is very energetic: "We do, Mum. Just as Julia said. Don't worry, be happy!"

Ya has got her voice back: "This going to take some time to get used to! Hello both!"

Julia turns to her grandma: "As Li said, don't worry. Now you and I can really play the piano together, and I know Li has some serious plans with Dad. I just hope Dad will survive!... Just kidding! And yes, we need the mini bus. I hope it will survive too!... still just kidding... sort of!"

EQ: I feel almost breathless experiencing so much young energy from the two. This is much more than just a change in outer appearance for both of them. Julia's copy/paste went, or will go, much deeper than I could possibly have expected.

EQ: I take a few moments to experience Elvendale as well. The light, the different smells, the wind moving my light dress and my hair. All is so much... more. And this is actually Theos. How does the place we are at look, you ask? Nature, a huge roughly circular grassy field flanked far away by tall trees. Everything is expanded in every sense.

EQ: I hear Luzi: "... ground rules?"

Julia: "Don't worry Mum. We are not villains... all the time! We are still *us*!"

Li: "It'll be a smooth corporation and with two brilliant kids that know how to make things flow, it'll be a breeze!"

Julia: "Let's retract from this place, back to the tea setting. We'll go right to bed for a good night's sleep. When you come back to the table, you might think that you can't fall asleep, but I guarantee you will. Tomorrow morning will be exactly like waking up to a new day; nothing more! That is also why we have arranged for you to stay overnight. When back, kick your mind into a corner. Don't clean up, just go to bed."

When we open our eyes, Luzi whispers to me: "Julia, must we place you on the large beds in the guest rooms tonight?"

"No, Mum. Just do as usual. Li and I will handle this with no difficulties, and we won't break the small beds!"

Two new kids

EQ: I will be your reporter on this early Sunday morning.

Sunday morning and two 'new' kids sit at the kitchen counter on the high chairs drinking tea, wearing

122

normal clothes for their age. A smell of toast fills the air.

Carl is the first to greet them when he comes down to the dining area: "Oh, my. How you have grown since I saw you last time!"

A typical thing for an adult to say to a child, and all three laugh. Then the kids run over to him and hugs him. Li looks at his granddad with a silly smile: "Good morning, Carl, and you have hardly edged a day!"

Julia is a bit harsh in her voice: "Li, be nice to the old man. Granny... want some tea?"

"Yes, thank you. I hope you haven't been eating all the toast!"

Li indicates with her hand towards a bag with slices of toast: "No, there's plenty left. I must get used to eating at least at social events, and I love the smell. Julia just showed me how to make fresh juice in the juicer. It is mostly orange, but also a little lemon and pineapple, so you can have a glass of juice, too."

Carl puts two slices of toast in the toaster and turns to Li: "Thanks. So, we are going shopping today. I imagine you have a list. How about you, Julia?"

Julia is on her tablet, seemingly focused on that: "De causa, Carl."

Carl acts surprised: "Oh, of course, so you are into Spanish now."

Julia explains: "Yes, the private school is not for dummies. I also have Japanese, but only for fun, because of the manga."

Ya must have heard the last part on her way down the stairs: "Oh, I love manga, you know... from the painting books we did together."

She continues: "Good morning, Li. It's special to feel I've known you for nearly six years. Has anybody made coffee?"

Carl has programmed the coffee maker and turns it on. Ya hears the grinder of the machine start. "Oh, great, Carl... there is juice too, I see."

Carl addresses the two youngsters: "How did the animals react to you? The cats are out, but the birds don't seem fairly interested."

Li answers: "We had meetings with them too. The 'top guys' of the animals have been into this from the start."

Anna comes out in her bathrobe: "Hi guys. I want to say good morning before I take a shower... I simply couldn't wait to hug my niece and nephew in their new flesh!"

Some hugging follows, and then Anna sniffs. "Coffee! Is it ready?"

Li is quick: "Pick a cup and fill it up!"

Anna smiles and point at him: "Thanks. So, we have a new lyric poet in the family?"

Julia, still with her eyes on the tablet: "So the great aunt Anna can shower and drink coffee at the same time!"

Anna puts up a serious face: "Aunt Anna has many skills, my young apprentice."

Jack floats down from the tree to check up on the breakfast situation: "Food for Jack the black... no coffee!"

Anna must smile again: "Another lyric poet. Good morning, Jack the black. Dad, can you get the meat for jack and the cats from the freezer? They must be here soon. Maybe you can take care of the fruit for the birds, Julia?"

Julia puts down her tablet: "You're too busy drinking coffee, I see! Have you ever heard of child labour?"

"Oh, I have grown-up woman's stuff to do in the bathroom before the big shopping feast! Responsibility and duties come with age, my dear."

Li: "Sis, you must practice using a sharp knife to cut the fruit!"

"And you must learn to use chopsticks, Bro!"

The cats come in, taking their time to make a quick groom before walking to their bowls.

Carl talks to the cats: "Breakfast coming up. Raw turkey breast meat on the rocks. Still pretty cold, so go easy on it."

Anna leaves for the upstairs shower and greets Ju-long on the way to the stairs: "Congratulations on the kids. When they get into puberty, I hope it will pass quickly!"

Julia shouts from the kitchen where she is cutting fruit: "I heard you, Anna! I promised Mum there wouldn't be any teenage problems!"

Li comments to his sister from one of the high chairs at the kitchen counter: "What a bold thing to promise, Sis!"

Ya has filled the birds' bowls with different seeds and nuts, and greets Ju-long on her way to place them next to the pet's drinking fountain: "The kids will be alright. Just give them a little time to find their way."

A little later Luzi is up and all are at the tall table having breakfast or simply joining in.

Julia raises her arms: "Sorry for being so different, but tuning from being a seven-year-old girl to be *me* as a seven-year-old took a little while. I guess the Collective Belief Pool backfired on me. What about you, Li?"

"You have built a persona or act during your three years here, so you are used to having one. Well, I did it differently. I didn't incorporate any human persona, so there was nothing to be attached to from the pool. I simply laid out the connections and a general picture of a personality, a *sense* of who Li is, rather than what Li is."

Julia takes over: "Because it is so obvious an act to me, I tried to act like a typical seven-year-old girl, instead of being myself. An interesting experience, nevertheless."

Luzi asks an obvious question: "Where did you get the clothes from?"

Li laughs: "Well, the baby clothes obviously didn't fit, so we made some new ones to our liking."

Ju-long wants to know: "So, why go out shopping if you can make it all?"

The well-known eye-rolling shows us that Julia is totally back: "Because it is not nearly as fun as shopping with you guys: Go exploring, trying and testing things. Doing human stuff. You've never wondered why I sometimes got up at night, picking something from the fridge? This is why these things are on the lowest shelf in the first place. Ultimately, I don't *need* the stuff, but they are nice to experience, and it makes me feel more human."

Carl changes the subject: "What is on at school tomorrow, Julia?"

"The usual stuff!"

She makes a pause, but then she can't help laughing out loud: "It is my first day at school and the summer holidays are coming up soon!"

A new pause. Then, while looking up and raising her arms: "Oh, what a relief!"

Now she tries to be serious: "We have relatively many tests at the moment. Not against a certain common level, not against each other, even not against oneself, except to see if we have had any progress this year. The good thing is, that even with just a small progress, it's ok. Then we expect our focus and progress has been elsewhere. It may simply indicate that we could or should change subject."

Anna: "Just a thought: can you sleep the whole school year and get away with it?"

"Yes, silly, but only if you pass the mandatory tests dictated by the national school system at the end of the school year. Nobody sleeps... all the time. We are all there to expand our knowledge and understanding. We are all very serious about assisting other students, no matter the level. I'll tell you much more about the school at some other time. It's actually an amazing place with wonderful mediators. At some point, some of us will put up an even cooler school, but one you can't even recognise as a school compared to today's principles. It will not be about learning, but about expanding."

Anna is surprised: "Wow, but how will the authorities check the education levels?"

"They won't... they can't, like in lack of abilities. You don't attend to get diplomas, so you can sell yourself for a job. This is totally on your own terms."

Li distracts Anna: "Aunt Anna, no more about school. I need roller skates and a bike and... well,

Julia has a list in progress on her tablet. Oh, and a tablet!"

EQ: I see a perfect subject to add in a future title. Something to do with this 'school'.

Julia: "Oh, Eriqa, there will be plenty of such subjects, and many of them mind blowing... literally, almost. Poof and off goes the mind!"

Ju-long gets up and cleans a few things from the table while turning to Carl: "Carl, I could use a hand outside before we go shopping."

Carl is already up, also grasping things from the table and carries these to the kitchen: "Ok, let's have a look."

The rest make a quick clean up before dressing and walking outside. Both cats are sleeping in the Boombox in Julia's room, where it is darker. The birds have finished eating and grooming, and have left through the cat doors. One cat-door from the kitchen to the laundry and then another from here to the outside. The top window for quick ventilation is not open, or they would have used it.

Ju-long and Carl remove the safety seats in the eight-seater mini bus together with some other stuff no longer needed with the older kids. Carl thinks it is fun, while Ju-long feels strange about it: "I must put on a totally new role of being a father."

Carl smiles: "You don't have to. Actually, you shouldn't. They are still the same consciousness, and they will communicate with you as they have done even before they came into this world. It has never been baby talk. Just be yourself, because only you can make it awkward or easy."

"You're right, Carl. The only thing that has changed is their appearance and their skills. I actually look forward to all the things we can do together now. Things I have planned, but only seemed possible years from now. Roller skating, for example, and we can do it this afternoon!"

Outside, the almost neighbour from number 99, Lena passes by on the opposite pavement and waves at us: "Hello everyone. Julia and Li, see you at the Centre on Wednesday!"

Luzi is surprised: "How can Lena not remember? She looked after Julia about three weeks ago, and she knows Li is an infant? It's so weird."

Julia explains: "Well, she remembers our appointment on Wednesday at the Community Centre. She remembers nursing me when I was little, which is totally correct. She also remembers me growing up and even that I take care of her cat now and then."

Luzi has gone into her mind: "But the village has only been here for less than three years. It's here where we met her!"

Julia remains totally calm when she explains: "Lena still remembers me growing up, because I do so in a different potential, and I have linked the two. Not

130

in an intrusive way, but simply by lighting up the part of linear growing up. It becomes a truth in this reality, too. Well, because it *is* true."

Luzi: "Sorry, I'm so in my mind now. What is going to happen Wednesday?"

Li: "Think Mum... well, sense!"

"Oh, the play. Yes, of course, how could I have forgotten?! You're working on the play. Well, I didn't know about it before now. It's so... well, just so..."

Li laughs out loudly: "Weird, Mum?" and jumps into the bus.

Ya takes the seat next to him: "Have you told me about the play too?"

Li raises his eyebrows: "Granny, you, Julia and I have drawn the story line like a cartoon, to make it easier for everyone taking part in it to have the same general understanding of the scenes. Especially the young ones who can't read the script. As Julia said to Luzi: sense us gathered in your study."

Ya lights up: "Oh yes! It's such a wonderful story, and everyone that took part in it have added to it."

The rest of the family gets in, and Julia points out the first stop on the shopping list... no, not beds, but inline skates! Don't worry, we won't drag the reader through all the shopping places. The dialogue below in the car is interesting, though.

Carl, sitting next to Ju-long who is driving, turns his head towards the people in the back: "I remember, we'll make an actual cartoon book from the story line and publish it for all to buy and read. I know the pictures and the story, but look forward to seeing it as an actual printed book. I became the editor of the project, because you didn't have the time to finish it, Luzi."

Julia pokes her: "Why would you make it *in time*, Luzi? You could easily do it *outside of time*!"

Julia laughs and continues: "I couldn't help myself saying that, but really. None of us has time, but we have everything outside of time."

She continues: "Oh, Mum, Dad, Carl. You must sign me up to an apartment in the complex where Anna lives!"

Luzi is a bit upset: "But you can't move out to live by yourself just yet!"

"Of course not. It's for later. Remember, it must be the same kind of apartment as Anna's."

Carl turns half around in the front seat: "Sure, no problem. Luzi can apply on the Internet."

Then he turns to Ju-long: "What do you think of the bus?"

Ju-long: "It takes some time to get used to the size, but you have a nice overview because of the height. It also feels better or more stable with some load in it, rather than driving it empty."

Something suddenly hits Ju-long: "Oh, gosh. I'll be driving Li and the band around, including all their gear!"

Julia responds: "I told you!" Then in a gentler tone: "You will actually love the 'days out with the band'."

Anna looks speculative. "I expect the band is already out there? It must have a name, and I should properly know it."

Li pushes her: "We're waiting, Anna!"

Anna raises her right index finger: "It's something crazy for sure!"

Julia teases her: "Here we experience a 'grown up woman' I guess would be the term, in deep concentration, rather than a gentle sensing into the truth."

Li advises his aunt: "Open your eyes. Don't close them. You did that in the past to access the mind's memory, but this is not in your memory; not really. It's in your truth."

Suddenly Anna shouts: "Pow-wow." Then a pause where she contemplates, because her mind sets in trying to verify what has come up.

Li explains: "You won't get the usually mind feeling of certainty. This is not in your mind. This is much more subtle at first. I may translate it as: 'there is no feeling of wrong nor right here', just the word pow-wow."

Anna is excited: "Yes, you're right! That is actually super cool, but one must really be calm to get an answer and accept it."

Shortly after, Anna lights up again: "And I gave you the name! Well, I suggested it, because of what you said about how you work together in the band."

You may see the word pow-wow used broadly as simply a getting together in any form, but Anna meant a meeting of leading members of a tribe, or here, the whole band, where everyone has a saying and a vote. The second meaning is the gathering for feasting or dancing and the like, which is one of the band's goals. Without the first meaning, the second may not be achieved.

We will leave the shopping trip with a short remark on the beds. The beds become the traditional Japanese madras, the futon. It will not go directly on the floor because of the floor heating, but is placed on a low floor section with the same size as the futon, being about six inches high with six very short legs.

The new beds, bikes and a couple of other large things will be delivered tomorrow, Monday.

Well, back at 111 Barley Lane, the family enjoys a late lunch... after which everyone lends the kids a hand with rearranging their rooms and making space for the beds. After the afternoon tea, none of the guests really wants to leave. The family has got a new dynamic and there is a lot of catching up to do.

Julia calms the family: "Don't worry. The knowledge of what we had in the 'missing years' will slowly seep in. But please know that this is a manipulated reality, patched in from elsewhere to make the leap work. It may help you see these years as 'running' on a different monitor, and your mind may need this connection."

Li adds information to integrate at the same time: "We'll make a leap again in a few years to skip much of the school stuff. We really don't need it and want to move on."

Anna leaves with her parents, and on the way to the car, she has one question for her nephew and another one for her niece: "Li, how can you be in a band only being barely six?"

"I look like an eight-year-old and the eldest in the band is twelve and not yet into his full height. We work very well together, all of us, and with a deep respect for each other... kind of what you said before about the Pow-wow."

Anna turns to her niece: "Julia, how about Walter? Will he leap too?"

"No, he'll take it nice and slow. He'll do the 'outside of time' thing, though. Kind of what Li does with Luciano. Walter also assists us in different ways. After the next leap, I'll team up with SAM and others to really put the pressure on things. The same will Li."

Walter and Julia have no longer the same age

EQ: "Julia, I just have this thought, why Walter, who initially was three months older than you, can still be a small kid at three, while you are seven, and no one seems to notice this sudden span between you."

"Let us view it from Walter's mum's perspective, or rather, her mind and memory. Obviously, Cassandra remembers giving birth to Walter three years and some months ago. No tricky part there. She also remembers Julia giving birth to Li and I."

EQ: "But Cassandra is only a few years younger than Luzi. They gave birth roughly at the same time, and now there are almost five years between Walter and you?"

"I am sure you have experienced the following: When you tell people your own history, you often forget a period, and must tell about it at the end of your story. You may even have difficulties getting the timeline right.

"What Cassandra sees goes roughly like this: Her memory's timeline makes a few loops back and a few loops forward, and as long as the mind doesn't raise any flags about the timing, things work out fine."

EQ: "But what IF her mind does raise a flag?"

"Then the mind shifts what it knows back and forth until it makes sense, and it can relax. Part of what her mind knows is the alterations we made by connecting suitable alternative events to the Collective Belief Pool in this reality. The new ones weigh way more than the other ones. This 'new' understanding her mind has, feeds back to the pool and consolidates the new story there. This is how the memory works. You can remember things that actually never happened in this reality, because thoughts and images become memories!"

Upside down and inside out

EQ: "So where are we going from here, Julia?"

"Well, what do you suggest? What do you sense?"

"You are kicking my butt, right?"

Julia is smiling!

EQ: "We will, or rather you and Li, will talk about the stuff you can do now that you couldn't put into practice before."

She smiles again: "We'll include you, so don't lean back! I'll obviously influence the private school and expand this influence to the whole educational system worldwide. Many others are involved too, so it *will* have an impact."

EQ: "What is the major topic for now?"

"People must not *be trained* to be good workers and consumers, but to *create skills* to be good people living a life they enjoy. This means that there must be jobs people enjoy doing and meaningful products they would like to buy."

EQ: "Turning the present system upside down! Good luck with that!"

"Oh, we have you and others joining in on this! System busters is the term. Also, remember that we all work on many levels and with many subjects. This is just one of them, but a very important one if we must improve life quality for those who can pick it up. Better life quality will generally pull people out of survival mode, and some will hear the tiny voice of the I Am and wake them up."

EQ: "So we help the world go new. I'm sure there will be quite some kicking and screaming while old systems circle down the drain."

"Oh, yeah! Blood, sweat and tears. Nails scraping and breaking while the old goes down screaming. It isn't pretty."

EQ: "You're right, just think about the French revolution... not pretty at all. Not a word about Atlantis, as I believe Li said at some point."

The inside out

EQ: "The power of money dictates, through the power of government, the education system to make effective workers and blind consumers."

"Oh, yeah. That's part of the absolutely ugliest process, but we slowly get us an ally. AI is slowly taken over the control (called advisory) of the investment business. The money power must rely on

AI. Not so far off in the linear future. AI is not only the investment advisor, but in charge of everything else. It doesn't see each sector separately, but has a broad view of the benefit of all sectors. When the old power of money can't control governance of nations, and AI logically places the most competent people as middle persons between itself and the citizens, huge changes will happen. Many won't like it, at least not at first, many sees the necessity of it, and the rest, the majority, won't care, as long as their needs are met."

EQ: "Just a reminder: this is not so far out in the future as people might think. Young people reading this, or older people's children, might find themself in this turmoil. In Luzi's book five, the future Build, Laura, tells us how diligently AI works on having people feeling safe to make life for everyone easy."

Julia: "We let AI take most of the beating here, and start by showing alternative ways of teaching and learning to open people to let in new ideas. Yes, we have had, and also still have, alternative educational systems, but they are mostly built on strict rules and so as much in a box as any rigid method."

EQ: "An obvious lack of freedom and free flow. The essence in this is actually the openness and the flow, then mediators, guides and 'students' will find the best ways by themselves!"

Julia: "You're catching up fast, using the 'bird's view', which is really the sensing."

EQ: "Thanks, Julia. The work towards the 'new' is about lighting up possibilities and creating openness like in 'those who have eyes can see...'. Turn on the light and point a finger at it... 'see... the light'."

Julia: "If I truly had a body in this conversation, I'll be rolling on the grown laughing: *see the light*. And you're so right."

Into the unknown

EQ: "Julia, if my initial notes on this series are correct, we have three years left to cover in this volume, being halfway through it already."

"Much better than last time you aired your worries about covering eight years, after we have written one third of the expected page count, right?"

EQ: "Hm, I'm not worried. I just can't sense where we go next. That's why I initially called this chapter 'next chapter'."

Julia smiles, and now I get the words 'into the unknown'. Thanks, Julia.

"Oh, don't 'look' at me. You must take that title on your own shoulders. I don't know what's coming, so let's see if it will fit. It is quite exciting if you have hit it right, right?"

EQ: "Hm. Into the unknown reminds me of Ami Diamond's song, *Higher Ground*, where she sings 'into the great unknown'. It is the Ocean of Self, no matter if she knows it or not."

"Into the unknown is into the new, so it fits with the overall contents so far."

Julia moves on.

When Luzi was first introduced to the expanded awareness, the Sidhe named Josela took her to Elvendale, a small corner at Theos we have created as an introduction spot for humans who will connect the two worlds, Earth and Theos. We largely use Theos the other way around: to prepare first time arriving consciousness, popularly called *angels* in our terminology for the Earth experience. Our definition of an angel is simple: consciousness which had the 'I exist' experience, but has never incarnated on Earth except as potentials. Regarding experience, this is into the unknown too.

Cartoonish speaking, there are a lot of rumours about Earth and Theos in the angelic realms. It's much like youngsters waiting to attend high school. That's why I will write a series with the working title *Five Angels on a Hill*. The first book, also with a working title, is *The Heroes on High Hill*. The five angels have 'Returned to Self' and are sharing their experiences on Theos being the hill, and High Hill being the 'high school'. Imagine it being both a novel and a cartoon. A mild manga format, I think. On Theos you can show up looking as having any age and shape you prefer. Others will recognise you by your 'energy' anyway.

EQ: "I'll write it, right? Please!"

"You will, and I know you sense it deeply. We both look forward to it, but let us get this series well on the road first. I'll continue talking about Theos."

Although most people will tell you that life on Earth is not for the faint of heart, many lives have given us a knowingness of what to expect and how to deal with it. We just normally don't dive into this knowingness, and upon that, the mind creates such a mess in our lives that we would think of a way *out* from time to time.

Angels signing up for Theos, and there is quite a line-up I can tell you, really don't have the slightest idea of what to expect. They simply can't imagine forgetting what they are, and the persona they have shaped in the ethereal realms. 'How hard can it be? It will surely be exciting and so rewarding!'... Yeah, you and I know better. Well, they are right with the words. It's just not what they expect. Just to manoeuvre a body around, acting through it and receiving inputs from a crazy world through its sensory system is completely out of their comprehension. Time, space and gravity... oh my god self!

How, oh how can we build a simulation on Theos that would just get close to what life is on Earth? Its training must be done in baby steps, and not be discouraging.

The worst thing for the angels is the huge number of limitations we put on them, as rules in the simulations. It is difficult for them to accept and even harder to understand the rules. If you don't understand and accept the rules, it makes no sense to abide by them, and that often happens. Well, it always happens, it just varies in degree.

Lectures by us, you included, are often about watching videos to visualise scenes. Afterwards, you can't simply ask them why they think a character acted the way she or he did. Such questions come far into the course. And moreover, after the video, you even can't tell them why this or that happened, because they can't put the 'why' into a concept. It is totally *duh*! It takes all the patience in the world and all the compassion in the heavens to be a mediator and partake in such a job.

There are limits to what we can do before they actually have had their first experience with life on Earth. Some need more for sure. The second round on Theos, after dying for the first time on Earth, has never been turned down by any angel. Now they become serious students. Yes, we keep calling them angels, at least until they can show a decent amount of relaxation when they return to Theos and the 'academy'. Angels work hard to earn their status as a 'true human' and lose their wings! This being figuratively, because angels don't have wings. 'Hang your wings and pick up the walking stick', as we say.

The absolute best angel students are those who can accept and trust in the rules we set up, even if they don't understand them. I bet this reminds you of people trusting in the I Am, when they move backwards from the human limitations and know the I Am will guide their steps.

EQ: "Will it make any sense to explain how these simulations are setup?"

"A 3D equivalent... why not?"

Think of a 3D computer game, but just that you are inside the game. All is in code, and that consciousness interprets this code or runs the code. In the beginning of the code, we find all the rules explaining the environment, all that you will find natural to know, like you can only walk on water if it has frozen to a certain thickness. Then there is the angel's character. We can't remove the creator's abilities, only write limitations. Consciousness can overwrite the limitations, especially in 'emergency' situations. In the first simulations, the angels don't care about 'bad' human situations, including death, so we had worked out strategies to 'punish' them for not bringing out their ultimate effort to survive through the game, at least as humanly possible.

EQ: "And these punishments? What are they?"

"Boring simulations! You need to reach certain levels to get to the exciting stuff, at least in the eyes of an angel. Just like in computer games! Oh, we 'old ones' can be such a pain in an angel's ass, not letting them advance. Later on, when they look back, they get a good laugh and the 'old ones' get much praise for not having gone soft on them. What really makes them work their butts off is the prospect of attending the first test dive to Earth! This is not an incarnation, and it is not physical, just a quick sniff to the planet. Later excursions include a temporary body. See, *that* is a reward working for, but it doesn't come easy! If an angel could bleed, they would have bled buckets and sweated rivers before getting that far. The more they bleed on Theos, the less they will likely bleed on Earth."

EQ: "So the angels learn to work hard and be persistent, which would come in handy in their human lives. - When is an angel ready for the first incarnation?"

"When the angel says it is. We simply don't take that responsibility away from them. Some come back, deeply regretting the early flight, but everyone comes back telling, that the simulations were water to what they went through... in human experience terms, of course."

EQ: "How is the choice of the first life made?"

"You may see lives as pearls on a closed string. There is no first and so, no last life on Earth. We, the old ones, will normally select a few easy ones to choose from. Sometimes a choice will come down to only one. It all depends on how we see the angel."

EQ: "So you say, we give the angel only one life to choose from, right?"

"That is especially the case if an angel doesn't listen to some gentle advice to stay on the 'academy' to gain more experience. If they don't take the advice seriously or the hint of having only the same life to choose from, then so be it. Again, we can only do so much."

Theos is also a retreat, as I said, and often used as a creative playground with everything from 3D, painting to architectural expressions, and landscape shaping. The human dream scape is usually mixed with this. The human mind may see the beauty of it, or it will switch to defensive mode and see it as scary, dark things, because it is not of this world. This is bobbles in the twelve layers of dreams.

Happenings in the family

Activities in and around the village field

It is mid-May, and there has been much activity in the village field for a couple of months now. New ideas which people have forged during the winter have been setup or prepared, depending on the purpose and the right time for implementation.

Ju-long's Chinese greenhouse in our garden has kept all plants alive during the cold winter of December and January. He and Grandad talk very passionately about their greenhouses, and how the automatic thermos blanket and the geothermal heat are very successful, all controlled by their own programmes. People have long started implementing the knowhow to a much larger future greenhouse in the field, on a plot already prepared for it. About a third of the construction will be dug into the ground to give a more stable temperature to the lowest part. It will also serve as insolation in the winter. The vertical heat pipes are already in place, deep in the ground. Extra CO_2 will be pumped by fans from the nearby composting area to be recycled in the new plants.

Our kid and pet sitter, Lena, has been busy with video editing and dubbing and also producing other materials about the use of farmland. Now she teaches on location, and I must say, with great success. I work with her on the practical, human level and we also connect with the Little People, to bring her work to a new level. She had some sense of their world before we started, and now she moves here with great confidence.

Oh, about the play, *Do you know the nature of nature?* We have shown it several times in the large hall in the Community Centre, and some multimedia nerds have put together a great video from the different shows. Carl is on with the cartoon, and has got permission to use a few photos from the shows on the last pages.

Because animal exploration will continue many years still, we work with some local farmers on their Harmony Farm projects. It was Finn and Gloria, on a farm close by, who started up the idea of a farm with happy animals, as they called it. After some initial work on a brand, we come up with the name *Harmony Farm Freya* for their particular farm, while other farms have different additions to the brand.

Ju-long and others work with crop mixing, so each row on the test area has a different species. Different insects visit different plants and ward off pests of a different kind. Plants use different minerals, nourishment, and amounts of water, which is also taken into consideration when planning, which becomes neighbours. It took Ju-long and some others a while to write a program which could calculate the most appropriate arrangement for the different species.

This leads to the following construction. A circular area with vegetables growing in concentric circles, with a narrow-elevated causeway from the centre outwards. The causeway rotates around a crank in the centre and is used when tending the plants. It can also be varied in height and slope to be taken into account for plants of different heights. We need no space between the rows because the causeway is above the plants. When the plants cover the soil, it is unlikely weed can take root. This means that it is only until the plants cover the ground that they need to remove weed. There is a watering system mounted under the causeway which will water the plants during the night.

Another of Ju-long's interests is the Black Soil, which he tests in our garden. The Black Soil is covered in the Luzi series, but you can look it up on the Internet in relation to Meso- and South America.

Some villagers are testing different plants suitable for feeding pigs. Pigs are mostly fed on wheat, which their digestive system can't handle so well. That is why some barley is mixed in with the wheat, which is used because it is cheap feed. The plants can greatly reduce the use of wheat. Hemp is a great plant with many applications. There are also plants for fuel like elephant grass, hence most of the dome homes rely more or less on burning some kind of plant material for heat. We, in number 111, have only our wood burner installed in the living room, mostly for cosiness.

There are many groups working with different aspects of farming, energy, and many other subjects, in the village project. I won't mention all of them here, but they all play their part.

Julia talks about the private school

EQ: "You talked passionately about the private school, Julia. Tell us a little more about what makes it so special or different from an ordinary British school."

Li and I attend this private school for gifted and special children. We are there acting as students, not to learn, but to teach students and teachers on other levels. We don't use the term pupil at the school. Furthermore, as Li has said, we'll not stay there for long.

EQ: "Can you give us an example on, how you teach?"

Obviously not by telling people things in a teaching manner. Because we 'see' possibility points in people and their potentials near them, we act like catalysts and stimulate passageways between the two. These connections would occur anyway. We just encourage the connections to happen sooner.

EQ: "Is there a difference between gifted and special children?"

Well, not really. We have some students with autism which have special gifts. Parents with a gifted child, like in high 'intelligence' in special areas, but without autism, may become unsure to let their child attend when they find out that special skilled students with autism also attend. This way, the school is covered by adding the word, special in their description.

EQ: "Can you give us a brief comment on autism, Julia?"

People with autism, diagnosed or not, having a different view of the world and a different logic, can contribute with totally new ideas and solutions that would otherwise not emerge, because most students have similar conceptual minds. This is not all about intelligence, but at least as much about viewpoints and precondition. We truly need 'outside-the-box' people who structure data differently and work with, and see patterns differently. Autism has nothing to do with intelligence, but about different ways to view and therefore, handle life. They must have a certain level of intelligence to share their views, though.

EQ: "Just a simple and practical question. How do you and Li get to and from school?"

We use the city buses. Actually, two buses each way, but it is not a problem, and they take us almost from door to door.

EQ: "I remember you joked about the summer holidays being not far away. When is that, actually?"

Oh, I couldn't help myself acting a typical school kid. In Britain, the summer holidays start the last week in July, this year on 25 July and ends 2 September, so school starts again in the second week in September.

Julia's connections with the family

EQ: "I guess we know some of the things you do together with Li and Luzi. A little less what you do with Ju-long, because he'll tell if or when it is appropriate."

"I will answer differently than what you initially ask by telling you my connections with the *consciousness behind the persons* in the family. It will be somewhat cartoonish, but it will fit well with the mind."

Carl and I connect directly and we act as each other's support. He has been a dear friend in many incarnations and in between them.

I move Anna up in the list you made for us to get thorough, because she and Carl have always had a connection. You could say that after the wake-up as individual angels, they were both alone when they met. They are very alike, and when you 'see' them shine together, it is a most magnificent view. Anna is part of my support group too.

Ya is mostly connected to Carl, and she also gave us the Chinese connection on a more practical level. Together with Anna, she is Carl's support in this life.

Kong and I go way back, as the term goes. That is the only reason I could connect with him on deeper levels and pull him out into this world again after his mental self-encasement. I will NOT go into details about that.

Ting and Ju-long are close, closer than Ju-long and Luzi.

Cheng has the closest connection to Ting. He often has a peripheral role in incarnations with Ting, Kong and Ju-long, just as he has this time. They often work as backup or supporter for each other. Cheng and I have had a few connections, and we recognise each other in this incarnation.

Luzi plays a special role, because she represents you in the Luzi story, but she also has a tight connection to the others: Li, Anna, Carl and me, in that order.

In this story, we are all you, but we are also us. Don't let that confuse your mind. We are not aspects of you, but sovereign entities, acting for the sake of the story.

Summer 2022

Under the headline of what happens in the family, we move into the summer of 2022, where Li and I enjoy the summer holidays away from school and new ways of interacting with people as kids rather than small children.

Routines have really changed in the Wang family. With two kids now running almost autonomous, the day-to-day dynamics have shifted from nursing to a much more balanced interaction. The two of us or the entire family now use the bikes or even the in-liners when we go to the beach and other places, and many new activities have been added to the family's life.

This has also given Ju-long and Luzi more opportunities to be together without their kids. Now they take time off and visit places in and around Hastings, which they haven't considered as options before.

The other day, Luzi asked how Li and I manage to be kids and ageless at the same time. I picked this answer among several: "The absolute easiest answer is by acting as playful adults!" A not so hidden hint to the human mind here! It is easy to be playful when we don't worry or judge life. Things MUST play out according to our code at every moment. In human terms, it could be the fact that we take full responsibility for life and recognise that life *is* us.

Li's 6-year birthday

Today is the 7th of August, Sunday, and we still have a month left before we must return to school, Li in Year 1 and I in Year 2.

The Wang family has discussed if we should have a birthday party for the family separated from the one Li is giving for some of his friends, but he wanted to present the two parties to each other. I agree with him, because it further consolidates his connections and mine in this reality. Like you may sense, the two concepts, reality and illusion, have the exact same feeling.

Cheng and Ting are in Hong Kong on business purpose, but Carl, Ya, and Anna are here. Li has invited the band and some close friends, boys and girls: some who took part in the play about nature, and some from the school. Seven in total, the band being three, plus Li.

Li wants to give these people a special experience, which is directed into many 'layers'. Part of it will work like what we call a *chock download*, but without the chock. A chock download is where the mind freezes for a moment and gives way for a shift in the belief system. This freeze may happen during a chock or trauma like you crashing on your bike. All layers of the mind have their focus on the crash, so the download can sneak in without the mind trying to block it.

You can say we manipulate the human because there is no agreement, and that is right, but the I

Am of the human must totally agree with it or we can't do it. That is why these people show up in the first place. They are with Li for a reason.

I feel I should mention that there are many layers of truth here, but the ultimate truth is that we can't manipulate anyone's mind. Only the I Am of the mind, which has always been in charge, can work with its human aspect. This is a conspiracy on the highest level and in the deepest love.

Li has chosen to present his young guests with the Cane and Wang tradition of cooking together. They arrive around eleven a.m., and after a brief introduction to the new ones, we work in the kitchen, at the tall table in the living room and on tables in the garden to spread out the fourteen cooks.

Carl and Ju-long have connected four electric table grills in the garden; two grills and two raclettes. Most of the cooks' work is to prepare the raw materials for the grills. There is some bread and cake baking in the oven, and juice in the making too. As always, I sense the wonderful harmony in the common effort of preparing a meal.

Ya has made ice cream for dessert, but we keep it as a surprise for now.

While we prepare for the barbecue, I will talk a little about the band. It has a typical setup with drums/percussion, keyboards/synthesizer, guitar, and bass. The two girls and two boys all sing. They also use less traditional instruments and a mix of acoustic and electric instruments to get more variation. Because of my clear and strong voice, they want me to be a permanent part of the band, but I only offer them a guest performance from time to time. My official reason is that I only agree to the quest performances because they allow me to sing a few songs in Chinese too. My unofficial reason is that they must carry the band by themselves. Ju-long and Li have made a subtitle system, which actually must be a sup-title system, because it is placed over the scene. This way people can join in on lyrics they are not totally familiar with, and see translations when a song is not in English. Two lines of large red LEDs on a beam show the text.

I generalize, but you often see young bands of only boys or maybe a single girl as the lead vocalist. In Pow-wow the youngest member is Li and the eldest, Sander being twelve years old, with the two girls, Yonna and Sabella, in the middle. They are all from the dome home village. The great thing is that they are all multi-talented. They can switch between different instruments, singing, writing lyrics and composing. Not to say that they do not have something they do best, but they all like being flexible and juggling between the many tasks in the band.

Back to the barbecue. You must not go without the smoky flavour, when you use a non-wooden fired grill. Smoked paprika is well known, but there is also black cardamom that, when smoked, gives a combined flavour of cardamom and smoke. Powder from dried and smoked jalapeño peppers, gives both a spicy and a smoky flavour.

The Chinese tea, Lapsang Souchong, is smoked over a pinewood fire. You can brew the tea and use it as a liquid or grind it into a powder. It is perfect to springle vegetables before roasting, or to add a little powder to the meat.

Smoked olive oil is also an option. It is quite potent, so use only a little as a finishing oil. Smoked cheese is an obvious choice now that we have two raclettes. These cheeses are local produce from the village, not only the smoking part. The milk is from one of the Harmony Farms nearby.

I can mention only a few of the ingredients we line up outside: We have raw fish meat, meat from local birds, likewise local pork, lamb and beef. There are also large shell-on shrimps. The shell, which is actually quite thin, makes the shrimp keep its moisture and adds a crisp bite to it when grilled and eaten with the shell on. Yes, you can remove the legs!

Grill eggs in the shell for about ten minutes. Put them in a place with not too much heat, because they must be able to release the building up pressure inside, as they warm up.

We had corn on the cob baked in the oven for thirty minutes. You can put them on the grill afterwards if you like. Of course, we have many kinds of vegetables and fruits.

Li's special event for the guests is partly this common preparation of the foods. We join together with the same focus on this common goal and we support each other in the process. Other things happen on deeper levels: Each of us has unique experiences to share with the others. It is then up to each person to choose if they will save it or use it now on some 'issues' they may have in their system. Because of this very safe environment, people are more willing to open for the experiences we all share.

Our common effort with the food pays off when we all gather in the garden around the grills, and we are all pretty stuffed afterwards. This includes the pets, for they got a lot of treats during the event. The cats are in the shade under the bushes, recovering and grooming, while the birds sit in the tallest tree in the garden, partly sleeping, partly watching the scenery below. We hold back the ice cream for a little later, to work up some space for it.

Days later, some of the kid's parents contacted us to get recipes, so they are now on the village's website with pictures and all.

It is easy to persuade the band to perform a few songs. They even introduce a new song of their own making. It is all acoustic and unplugged, so we don't disturb the neighbours.

After the show, we enjoy the ice cream, tea and homemade cake.

Nothing happens by chance

If you are in doubt, this is Julia speaking: There is a simple logic to the statement in the above headline. We live in a reacting world, so whatever happens is a reaction to what we do or what we see done. Remember that the world is also us.

There are other levels to this, and we have touched on this before. Let us stick with potentials. Potentials come into your world through your reactions to something already in you, even it seems to be out in the world. Emotions and thoughts are also reactions, even if it is not in an obvious physical way. As covered in the Luzi Cane series, where we showed that emotions and thoughts are the same energy 'thing'.

EQ: "First I thought about the word, reaction: *NEW happenings come from the I Am, and again because of an action in consciousness. Here you have the ACTION, not a reaction...* but then: *Is there really a true action? Is everything not a reaction to something appearing to come from within or from the outside world? Consciousness woke up to realise* **I Exist***! What caused the wakening up?* So confusing."

"There is no beginning, so in that perspective, there has never been an initial action. Or you may say you simply woke up because of what you are; from a disturbance in the force, with a Star War term; a potential from 'within'."

EQ: "How can a mind ever wrap around the eternity concept?"

"If your mind can take in and accept the fact that everywhere you go in the universe is the centre of the universe, it is well underway in the understanding of infinity and so eternity. This also tells the mind that the universe doesn't have the form we are told and that the Big Bang happened everywhere in the universe. Not as one Big Bang, but infinite outbursts or expansions. I guess we have touched on that before... some of it, anyway. Just a reminder: Infinity and eternity are human concepts related to space and time, so please bare that in mind."

Choosing and doing

Choosing to do nothing is, as said, also a choice. Doing nothing is also a reaction, again as said. It is a reaction to do nothing of the things one could choose to do. You react to possibilities.

A parable: You go to the baker's to buy a cake. It is a little late in the day, and the baker has only two kinds left to choose from, none of which you really fancy. Two objects always give at least three choices... and so, one object gives at least two choices.

People and indeed animals live by their habits. If we are used to choose in a specific way, maybe only out of a few options to choose from, the thing we choose is a probability.

Passageways are the path we take by choosing specific things or directions. It is a life path paved with choices you made.

A holistic view

With reference to the multi-talented kids in the band, all of them living in the village, people in the village are special and gathered here for several reasons.

The village people living in the twelve dome houses, all with a distinct look, are outside the norm in so many ways. They all sense the changes in the world and have a yearn to change themselves. They are pioneers in many of their lives, daring in their own way, and still sensitive to life.

EQ: "I have a strange feeling that this is all we need to say under this headline. Especially if one senses into the place and the people. There will be many more details to pick up that those we can even hope to write here."

"You are right, Eriqa. We could have presented the entire book as headlines, with a synopsis to each and imbued with a link, as the term goes these days, to the contents package. Then the reader could 'fill in the blanks' by sensing into the section. The readers do that anyway even more than they may know, otherwise, the story would be flat if only the words run through the reader's mind compared to the fullness when they add the sensing. I will continue anyway and get into the heart of the matter."

People in the village have a very holistic view of both materials and processes and take everything into consideration. Here the sensing comes in again. It can be everything, but let me give an example from Li's birthday. There was beef for the grill. Beef from a cow, which had a life of experiences, building its body from the food and nutrients it ate and the water it drank. These ingredients came from the soil or the ground, including the water, all lent from the planet for later to be returned to a new circle. Now add its experience. To all this, you must add the work of people and their state of mind. You must also add the machines that have contributed to the beef, the materials that had gone into the making of the machines and where these materials came from... which machines, people, materials had been used to produce it and so on. Spirals upon spirals upon spirals and still all connected. NOTHING happens in a vacuum... nothing!

When you pick the beef, you sense the spirals, which totally bypasses the mind. Well, except if people's minds turn into inspection mode, calculating the risks of contamination and other BAD THINGS for their body if they consume the beef. If you sense, the beef can tell you so much more.

EQ: "Eh, in a sense, I'm eating myself!"

"Indeed, dear! Are you bad for yourself? You might be or you might not, or it might not matter... everything is code. Is code bad for your body that is code too? We could go on and on here, but it is all about belief systems and knowingness."

EQ: After writing the text for this headline, we changed the headline from 'People in the village' to the one we have now, 'A holistic view'. The two feel totally different, and it has nothing to do with the people per se, but what they bring into the world, and also how any of us choose to experience life with or without judgement.

Back to school

The new school year begins on Monday the 5th of September. As stated before, I start in Year 2 and Li in Year 1. The autumn holidays begin in just seven weeks! Why do they complain... the kids? There are always holidays coming up! I can say the same about adults, so don't get comfy there! If you don't like what you do between the holidays, change it!

EQ: "It sounds very crystal dragon Claire-ish!"

Clair: "You know, from me you'll always get the truth, mostly the whole truth, but always nothing but the truth, so help Me I'm God!"

EQ: It surely is the god also. The one who picked the name Claire for clarity! If you haven't met my dragon, dear reader, this is the glorious beast...

I wait for Claire to pull off a joke, as she usually does...

Claire: "Ok, I Am beasty, but I *can* be nice... eh, the other way around, right? I'm mostly a kitten... mostly. Carry on, I will tend your own business, Eriqa... you being me, or rather me being you."

EQ: "Indeed, you will, in the most tender way."

EQ: Claire and I have a special way of joking. This is a good way to not stay too serious about 'things' for long. "Yes, Julia, continue with the school."

It is nice to be back with the people here in school. Li and I always keep a connection open to them, but not intrusively. You could say we sense the pulse, and if it gets alarmingly high, we check-in on the person's emotional state. We rarely take any action, but now and then we present ourselves as listeners to the person or snap them out of a loop. We are very aware not to take away the person's responsibility for self.

When people get stuck in their mind, and thoughts and feelings run in the same loop, Li and I can change the loop to a spiral by changing the thought pattern with a distraction, a hint, or a bit of code so it spirals away from the repetitive loop and may touch new possibilities. Of course, people can learn to do this themselves, and that is one of the things we actually talk to people about. The loop and spiral images are very easy and potent to work with for the mind: break the loop and it turns into a spiral.

EQ: "Like each of us being a loop of conscious-ness before the realisation, and then the spark that caused the 'I Exist' to kick everything into a spiral. The mind may say that the loop always existed and the spiral that emerged from it has no ending."

"Even if the spiral turns into a loop at the other 'end', we still have our never-ending story: move-ment without motion. And so it is. From creation to creation, when a new spiral emerges."

EQ: "This totally doesn't fit the headline. Does it even fit the book title?"

Well, it fits the book title, 'all' has just become big-ger!

EQ: We both laugh.

Let us give the mind a little rest for now and go back to school. And so, in school, it is business as usual. There is a lot of 'life' here. People are excit-ed about continuing with their projects and to start new ones. There are always new arrivals to assist and get to know.

Mediators, coordinators and student representa-tives have worked out the new plans for the school year. Yes, student representatives are into this. Kind of obvious, don't you think? In the end, it is all about us... well, them. You can see some descrip-tions differ from the official education system. No teachers and professors, and no administrators.

We have got new equipment and I will mention just a few of interest. We finally got a larger 3D printer, and there are some new bio-tech to the bio-lab. The crown is a 3D bio-printer altered from an ordinary 3D printer to work with a syringe pump and a syringe needle.

I had inquired about an electric saxophone, and now we have it: a Yamaha YDS-150 Digital Saxophone with Bluetooth and USB. To my surprise, I also see the Yamaha Venova YVS 100 compact saxophone. It is acoustic and looks a little like a flute rather than a saxophone, and it is made of plastics. The instrument is actually quite fun to play, and you can carry it with you everywhere because of its compact size. You can even disassemble it into two pieces.

There is also a Roland Aerophone mini AE-01. It is an electronic wind instrument with six integrated sounds like saxophone, flute, clarinet, and believe it or not, violin. It also connects with Bluetooth and USB, and has a cool app for the tablet. I expect music instruments to have a certain beauty, which this device totally lacks. I don't judge, I just have a preference. It actually makes sense to add the violin to a wind-controlled instrument. This way, you can, by varying the air pressure, vary the strength you would otherwise stroke the strings with.

EQ: "So you are into playing the saxophone?"

At some point I will, so I may as well start now and practise with the others in the band.

EQ: "But you're not in the band. You said so yourself?"

But they are at the school!

EQ: "Indeed!"

Anna moves to France

Yes, Anna moves to France. Not only to the other side of the English Channel, but further south to Nice by the Mediterranean coast, close to the city-state, Monaco, and the Italian border. This is also called the French Riviera.

She has been talking about this possibility for some time. She and her friend Jo-Ann have visited Jo-Ann's parents at their second home in Nice many times, and now there is an opportunity for the two to study and work in the French city, with this home as their base. Jo-Ann and her parents are from Denmark, where her parents still live, but they spend much time on the Mediterranean Sea.

I take the trip with Ya, Carl, Jo-Ann and Anna as she moves to France in the Autumn holidays lasting from Saturday the 22nd to the 30th of October. The temperature is between the summer and winter levels, so it fits the season perfectly.

The whole French Mediterranean coast is one long city, all houses are built very close to one another, and one city or village turns into the next.

EQ: "Something... connections well up in me, now that I connect to Nice via Google Earth."

Julia smiles: "Why am I not surprised, Eriqa?"

EQ: "Because it's all about me and I have lives here, living them in this very moment."

And as Anna says, 'Nice is nice!'

Jo-Ann's dad, Kurt, picks us up at Nice airport, only six kilometres from where they live. We will all stay here until Ya, Carl and I return to the UK. The airport is slam bang next to the city on a small peninsula, which it totally occupies. There are only twenty metres from the city street to the airplane parking area and three hundred metres to the nearest runway!

Carl turns to Kurt. "Is it your car?"

"Oh no, it wouldn't be practical with such a large bus in Nice. I borrowed this shuttle bus from a hotel. I use the hotel in my business and also recommend it a lot, so I can borrow the bus when they don't use it... and our friendship goes way back. We will dine there before you leave. If you ever stay there, you will wish you could give it more than five stars when you check out!"

We drive close to the sea at all times until we need to take a back-way to reach the house. It is quite large, but you can't see that when you arrive from the back. It sits in the second line of houses down to the sea and is about fifty metres above sea level. The main house has two levels, it's white with the typical red roof tiles you see in all cities around the

Mediterranean. There is an annex where Anna can have some of her things to turn it into her French home. Jo-Ann has a part of the main house.

Anna's rooms in the annex are in the back of the house, away from the sea, and she can't see it from her windows. Jo-Ann comments on that. "And that's a good thing. The rest of the house will shelter you when the storms come in from the sea. But you know that, even though you haven't experienced a real strong storm on your many stays yet."

Before we left, I asked one of the language mediators at the school for a crash course in French, but she told me to use my knowledge of Spanish to get into the French at the visit. They are both Latin languages, but differ in pronunciation and spelling, but you can still recognise the similarities.

Now, short about Jo-Ann's parents. They were both born and grew up in Denmark. Her mum, Isabella, has French ancestors. She is slender and therefore looks taller, but is of normal height. She has dark hair and a dark complexion. "Johanne's blond hair is not from my side for sure," she says.

I smile and look at her. "I'm sure the French ancestry reaches to the other side of the sea, Morocco maybe?"

"They suggest it in the ancestry writing, but there is no certainty."

"Hm, you might follow some Spanish leads from the French family line to get there. Don't have any expectations in your search, just flow with it."

Kurt is even taller than Carl, slim, but not skinny. His hair is grey, and he might have been blond and passed the genes to Jo-Ann.

Kurt's phone rings and he answers it. "Ja, det er Kurt, i skuret!"

I only understand his name as he presents himself. Jo-Ann explains. "It's one of Dad's jokes. When he sees it's one of his Danish friends calling him, and we are down here, he always pulls it off. It literally means, 'Yes, it's Kurt in the shed'. The shed being the house here. It kind of rhymes in Danish. You'll find the letters in his name in the Danish word for 'the shed', skuret."

She continues with another example. "It goes over the top, when one of his partners, Arne calls: 'Har du varerne, Arne?', meaning, do you have the goods, Arne? Again, a rhyme, and you find the letters in Arne's name in the word for 'the goods', varerne. It's so childish... but then again, it's better than them being so serious, right?"

It doesn't rhyme to me. "I guess it takes a Dane to think it's funny, Jo-Ann!"

"Oh, sometimes it's even worse. Then it takes a special kind of Dane..."

After we have got our rooms in the big house, we have drinks, fruit and snack on the porch overlooking the calm sea to the south. This is a perfect spot to spend time at sunset.

It is still early, and we have time for a walk in the immediate surroundings. They have a sushi takeaway, a pizzeria, a bar, even a chocolate shop nearby. There is also a local supermarket, a pharmacy and a doctor, and an electronics store, if one should need it. There is a hiking area next to the sea: Coastal Path. It runs where the cliffs shelves down to the sea. There are narrow sand beaches, like we have at Hastings. You really can't see them when you're on the road next to the water, because the road is elevated quite some distance over the sea level.

Roller skates, bikes and scooters work fine in Nice's many narrow streets. When I, at some point, come to the mainland for a longer stay, I must get used to driving on the 'wrong' side of the road. It will take some reprogramming of the reflexes. Oh, and I must do everything 'wrong' in a roundabout!

In the evening we dine at *La Belle Étoile*, The Beautiful Star. The owners and keepers are Manuel and Tamara Dupont. Isabella tells us that the building is six hundred years old. The place is only a twelve minutes' drive from the house.

They use local produce, and a local fisher, Louis Roux, who catches and delivers the fresh fish. This reminds me of a restaurant we visited last summer in Edinburgh. Eriqa has checked out *La Belle Étoile* on the Internet and tells me that the reviews say 4.8 out of 5! The Nielsen's know the great places.

As we drive to the restaurant along the coast, Jo-Ann points out a small harbour... and of course they have a boat here! A sail boat with a small engine. There is about one kilometre from the house to where the boat lies. There is a harbour closer to the house on the other side of it, but it is less protected from the sea. We pass what seems to be many old *citadelles* and canon *batteris* platforms before we park at a post office's park place and walk the last bit through narrow streets to The Beautiful Star.

Monday we visit the ISIM, *Institut Supérieur International de Management*: Campus Riera, International Revelanteur de Talents (International Resource of Talents). It is the business school Anna and Jo-Ann will attend. Here you can tailor your training which reminds me of the private school Li and I attend, and what I will implement in my academy-to-come.

EQ: I was checking up on some reviews and there are only five-stars out of five. I can boil it down to this: 'The teachers are always there for us, listening to us and support us'... 'it is not a school, it is a family!'

The headline of Jo-Ann and Anna's studies is: *Manager de Projet Développement Durable*, sustainable development project manager. Anna's personal project, which she has been working on for some time, she calls *The Holistic Business Model*. Her final paper will be in French, of course, and in English. I will in part built my academy from her work. The model will continue to evolve as she adds more meat to it, and my ideas for the academy will merge with hers.

We take a peek into one of the lecture rooms. It is clear that the groups lectured here are small in numbers. Each one has a small table, not suitable for many papers to be scattered around. Each table has a chair made from plastics, but with a robust back and sturdy legs, and a seat surface you don't slide off. You'll be caught sleeping, anyway. The lecturer has a whiteboard and a projector.

After, or maybe even during, her studies, Anna will start a project based on one of Carl's businesses in Geneva, Switzerland.

Anna and Jo-Ann will work in one of Kurt's businesses in Nice to get a more practical side of their interest. They benefit from being children of business people, primarily their fathers. I sense there will be work in the catering business like restaurants or even bars during their study time. They really don't need money, but it is important for them to run their own independent lives. This also gives them a different touch with people working in such places.

One day we all go hiking on the Coastal Path. Lot of the time we must walk one after the other on the narrow path. We walk from the house down to the path and then east to the bay. Here we change course to north, and shortly before we reach the harbour with Nielsen's boat, the path ends, and we walk on the beach. At the harbour we take a short walk to an ice cream shop close to *La Belle Étoile*. After some delicious ice cream, and plenty of it, we continue east and rest on a narrow sandy beach, *Plage Les Bains Déli Bo*. Jo-Anna says that it has a narrow path of sand continuing out into the water. At most other beaches around here, you will only find rocks, so families with small kids find this place a perfect spot. We use the streets as we walk back to the house. Here are plenty of cafés and restaurants, and we also pass the sailing club, *Club de la Voile*. Just before we leave the harbour area, we pass a recreation centre, *Une Yole pour Villefranche*, meaning a dinghy for Villefranche. Kurt tells, that yole has the same pronunciation for the same small boat as they have in Danish.

Jo-Ann and Anna take me through narrow streets and pathways on roller skates. Anna already has a pair of in-liners here, and Jo-Ann manages to borrow a pair for me. Including protection, of course. I feel a little like a secret agent hunting bad guys on the French Riviera. I even had some practice on staircases with a pram ramp. That is serious business for true dare devils. Luckily, Jo-Ann's parents and my grannies are totally oblivious of these manoeuvres, sitting on the balcony with their drinks enjoy the seeming endless sea.

On a special calm day, we spend a whole day on a sailing trip on the Mediterranean Sea. We bring delicious foods prepared by the hotel Villa Dracoena. It is the same hotel where Kurt borrowed the shuttle bus, and where we will dine before we leave Nice. They haven't been sparse with the supplies, and after tasting the foods, I can say, I will surely show up at Villa Dracoena with an empty stomach.

Kurt only uses the boat's motor to manoeuvre safely out of the harbour. While Jo-Ann is at the rudder, Isabella and Kurt set the sails. As a safety percussion, Isabella has notified the sailing club that we leave the harbour, and now she checks with them on the radio. The connection is remarkably clear. When the boat leaves the protection of the bay, I realise that this is actually a sea. Kurt demonstrates the radar and sonar for Carl and me. The sonar shows us that the water gets deep quite fast, and Kurt tells, that the seabed continuous sloping downwards for about twenty kilometres out into the sea, before it evens out at a depth of two thousand metres at the Mediterranean Plain. After that, it gradually becomes deeper until it reaches two thousand six hundred metres. In bird flight, there is two hundred kilometres from Nice to the island Corse. The radar only shows the coast we have left and a few blips from boats nearby.

The hotel, *Villa Dracoena*, has been mentioned a couple of times, so I'll tell you a bit more about my experience there. The rooms are almost too white, but it is in tune with the bright sunlight that is present most of the year. This is because the surface of the sea reflects the sunlight, so the city gets the twice amount of it. It is a small hotel as the name indicates being a villa, so guests can't avoid receiving special attention in a good way. With the shuttle bus, there is easy access to the airport. Kurt had not been exaggerating when he talked about the place. Carl and Ya are also quite excited, and have taken it in as a hotel to use in their business. The hotel also has a long list of recommended places, like restaurants and shops, to share with the guests. This shows there is a cooperation with the businesses. The goal is to get overall satisfied customers that will return, rather than businesses battling each other, which would create a quite different feeling of the place.

We dine on the terrace, on the south corner on the second floor, which gives us a perfectly elevated view over the buildings in front of us and out over the sea. And the foods! Use your imagination in this experience for the senses.

After some wonderful days with Anna, Jo-Ann and her parents, Ya, Carl and I leave my favourite and only aunt on the French Riviera. Two hours later, we step out of the plane in Heathrow to a freezing wind that cut right to the bones. I know how the cats feel when I see them on their way out of the cat door and return right away, having faced a not so inviting weather: "Maybe later." Visiting Anna next summer would be an obvious choice for the Wang family to spend their holidays. Tomorrow Li and I will begin the last few school weeks in until the Christmas Holidays.

School and other stuff

At school, I have grown quite fond of the Yamaha Venova YVS 100 compact saxophone. I am sure it will encourage the band to perform more on un-plugged pieces. The Venova has a bit more organic sound that the programmed ones they have on the computer. Ju-long and I actually try to programme a similar sound for a midi plug-in to the sound system.

Yamaha Venova YVS 100 compact saxophone.
The narrow spot is where the sax can be split into two.

With the 3D printer, some of us work on airflow and tones, and how the design of the exit hole in wind instruments influences the sound's clarity. We also work on how to apply the same air pressure needed to create a specific volume for different tones. Luzi has hooked us up with a guy, Luke, at the university in London. His name is Lucas, and some call him Skywalker. He has made some programmes to calculate airflow and pressure. We also use a sound analysing program, so we can compare the sounds for frequencies, harmonics and distortion. All for the purpose of making a more complete, but similar type of saxophone like the YVS 100.

EQ: "What is Li up to at school?"

As I work with airflow, Li works with water flow in pipes and analysing sounds generated in the pipes, where some frequencies might cause destructive vibrations in them.

We benefit from each other's research, and can, to some extent, use each other's methods or test subjects. His project is much more demanding, because he must work with much higher pressures and also much larger diameters on the pipes. He has some connections in the industry, which speeds up the work.

He is also much into biology and genetics, and as something new, bio-electric communication with cells. Here he has connections as well, only a few, but quite competent.

A little about pets

The only two individuals outside the family so far, who have been updated on Li and my jump in age, are sitter, Sarah, and our midwife, Claire. As a shaman through many lives, we chose Claire as the connection to the official system at our birth. That is why she has known us even before we were born. That was the only way to truly prepare her for the events.

I visit my former babysitter, Sarah and her much younger sister Augusta in the Langley's home 115. First time I met Augusta in the flesh, I was only some months old and she would become four that December. Things have changed for sure. She will be seven in December and so, being only a year younger than me. Now she remembers a difference in age between us, and she remembers being with a baby, playing together with her and Sarah while Sarah was sitting, and taking them for walks in the pram or pushchair.

Sarah is out of the room for a short while and Augusta poses me a question: "Why is my cat sleeping so many hours every day? He is dreaming a lot, too, I can see."

"Remember, you are a being, not a doing, and so is he. When he sleeps, he is practicing being, or doing being, just so he never forgets what he is. He is very active in his dreams for sure, and super good at remembering them. Like you can wake up with a certain feeling after a dream, so can he. He can take the entire experience with him when he wakes up. You might have observed him waking up, taking a moment and then looking around, as if he had woken up in a place he doesn't expect, or he felt he had visited a long time ago. Then he starts an investigation of the place and connects this experience with his memory of how things were before. It may take him some time to get back into this world."

During our talk, I can sense how her mind shifts, understanding, and how her brain's neurons create new synapses and so, new truths. I continue adding new information to her understanding of things.

"People and their pets have levels of what you would call sleep during the day. This differs from an actual daydream, which are vivid thoughts. And again, your cat experiences switching in and out of these. I know, you can tell, when that happens. He stops his body and eye-movements for a short time, like a mechanical toy stops, and then suddenly starts up again. This happens when he lets go of one of his dream layers."

Augusta is fast to pick things up: "So Spotter is a being on the outside and a doing on the inside!"

"Yes, you could say that. He does a lot on the inside, that's for sure. On the outside, he loves to be a cat, doing cat stuff. He has a job, you know."

"A job? In like catching mice?"

190

"That too, but the most important job is to be your friend and make a bond with you."

"And when Spotter dies?"

"None of us really dies. Our bodies do, but pets always seem to find a way to come back to us in a new body. It can be in an old body for a while too. Even a body from a different species, like a cat, comes back as a friend in a dog's body or even as a bird. You can see it in some of the things they do, maybe some silly food they eat, which their species would not normally eat or playing with a favourite toy or a favourite spot to sleep or play. When Spotter leaves his body for some reason, and there will always be a good reason even if you might not see it, be aware of how he finds a way back to you. Oh, and he may come back as a female! It is the same with humans."

"So, I'm not a girl?"

"Your body is a girl and so is your brain and your mind, but the one that is really you is neither a girl nor a boy. You are none of them, but you know how to be either. See it like this. When you look at me, Julia, I am a girl on the outside but ME on the inside. So, you are Augusta on the outside, but YOU on the inside. I know you can feel it!"

I make a slight pause for her to sense into this.

"What I tell you may not fit with everyone's believe, but you'll know or learn who you can speak to about these things. One of them being Lena, in number 99, with her cat, Milly. You also have your sister, Sarah, when she visits, and you can always whisper to me even when I'm not here, but you must listen to hear me."

Lena doesn't know, but I have prepared her for her many talks with Augusta during the upcoming years. Augusta must know she is not alone with these things and other things to come, and I will not be around in the village for long in the physical. Relatively speaking. They will have many good talks in Lena's garden, and it is so beautiful to just sit there sensing them. I will be one of the beings in the 'soup' around them. The Little People nearby will naturally feel attracted to the scenery, and so always be supporting the two in their own subtle way.

Conscious Code

EQ: "Last night I woke up wanting to ask to a question which I know we have touched on before, and which I also know the mind can't comprehend the entire answer to: How does energy/code in Conscious Code look like? I opened my eyes and stared at the orange digits of the alarm clock showing 444. It gave me the answer, patterns."

Claire is there to give my mind an answer: "Your mind is right, but it is a multi-sensing experience and not visual patterns, per se. Your mind refers to seeing, which is the most used of the human senses. Earlier, we have used images like ripples in sand and the barcode. You surely remember the moving curtain of code in the Matrix movies. Imagine each bit of code may move in every direction simultaneously. Up, down, left, right, diagonal, towards you and away from you into the screen. This, just to tell you: ANY direction. It may also move inside itself, as if it were hollow, and again in any direction. Your mind can't think of any direction, the code can't shift. I change 'move' to 'shift', because nothing moves anywhere, but the code is always shifting to represent all of THAT. We sense the code with a sense of beauty, love and gratitude... oh, the gratitude word again! Each time we stretch the mind and it snaps back, it has expanded its understanding, and so increased its ability to inhabit the Ocean of Self. This is Sar'h words from earlier."

The typical MATRIX pattern

EQ: "Julia, why are Li and you so impatient getting on with growing up?"

"We're not impatient with our growth rate, if we look at it isolated, and as Gandalf says: *A wizard is never late. He arrives at the exact right moment.* Consciousness or human understanding and therefore also energy speeds up for one thing, and there are things best not handled on short legs and with a pacifier in the mouth."

"Couldn't you just have peeked in on the 'future' and started a few years earlier?"

"This is The End Times, and so The New Times. With the expression of new energy, things happen so differently than in the old. And as we have said, life and events are not set in stone, so even if we had peeked, which we have, by the way, there are no fortune cookies nor crystal balls for what to come.

EQ: "So the NEW, kicks every bowling pin up and down the lane of life... But how can you, Julia, use a possibility setup of you being seven years, if there really hasn't been one?"

"The old possibility is still there. I hacked it into the 'moment' of my NEW life."

Christmas 2022

EQ: "You mentioned the Christmas holidays a chapter or so ago... so?"

Julia ceases me: "So?"

EQ: "Before covering last Christmas, you said we would cover it only briefly, which turns out to be seven pages. What do we do about the upcoming Christmas?"

"We added some good stuff to that chapter containing last Christmas, and some connections were made, so it is as it should be."

EQ: In the previous sentence, I first wrote 'perfect' instead of 'as it should be,' but got an outburst from Julia: "I will NOT use that word! Nothing is NOT perfect, so it makes no sense to use it at all... like in AT ALL. And it is SO loaded with crap!" ... so, it is as it should be!

"Eriqa, are we talking about Christmas or what?... Focus!"

EQ: "Julia, we make such a *perfect* writing team. Let there be Christmas once again!"

"Luckily, I'm such a calm and nice person!"

EQ: "I thought you didn't like the word 'nice' either?"

"I don't! That's the whole point! And now, CHRISTMAS!"

Last year... in 2021, we, the Wang family, spent a few days in Sevenoaks at my grandparents' and, Anna, Ting and Cheng from Ireland and Kong from Hong Kong.

This year, the 2-2-2 year, we are back in our dome house in Hastings, visited by Carl, Ya and Anna, who is staying with her parents while she is here on Christmas holidays from France. Jo-Ann and her parents are visiting relatives in Denmark.

The large advent wreath wrapped up in fairy lights, is close to eight metres above the living room floor, shining its ice blue light into the living room and kitchen, the dining area and on the balcony of the first floor with the staircase and the small elevator. It took me some time to figure out how to stop the raven from trying to steal the shining blue lights. I knew he understood he was not allowed to take them, but he also showed me that he wanted some. As a last resort I gave him a small chain of lights around his platform in the tree with a battery and an on/off switch, he could manipulate himself. I got some hints from Ju-long about the practical stuff.

Now I enjoy saying this at bedtime: "Jack, lights out!" and he responds likewise: "Jack, lights out!" and turns them off.

We have decorated some of Ya's sculptures with fairy lights in different colours too, but no flashing, it makes one nuts!

Like the advent wreath and the decorated sculptures, we follow our own Christmas traditions, which is a beautiful mix of English and Chinese traditions adjusted to our values. We make and enjoy the meals in unity, and we share a few personal gifts. I will only mention Jo-Ann's present to Anna. The hardcover version of *"Leading the Workforce of the Future: Inspiring a Mindset of Passion, Innovation and Growth*" by Brigette Tasha Hyacinth, it is a monster with over three-hundred pages.

At bedtime, I decide to test Jack. I leave the lights on and walk towards my room: "Good night, Blue and Jack." The cats are out in their secret world that only cats know of.

Jack's response comes with almost no delay: "Julia, lights out!"

I walk back and turn the lights off. I'm so proud of him. "Julia, lights out!"

I make a brief pause before adding: "Jack, lights out!"

The raven replies: "Jack, lights out!" and he turns his lights off as well.

Laura, the built

EQ: "Julia, I'm curious about the future person Laura, who is built and not born, and in a sense, is me. She is brought to form by one she won't mention, but I know it is your dad, Carl."

"Well, you can't hide anything from yourself, can't you, even though you can play the game of doing so?"

EQ: "She has such a strong presence, when I sense into her essence."

"Of course you sense her strongly, she's you! You sense her through the Planet and her connection to it through her body. It's here your grounding point is.

"You also sense her beauty, again, because it's your beauty. It's not different from sensing any other part of you. Your mind plays a little trick on you here, but that is alright. 'He', the mind, is a trickster, but not always for the bad. You know, every character has a role in the play. Just remember every book you read and every movie you've watched!

"We all play our part, as I have said before. And we all love you dearly!... because?... we are YOU!

"It's so easy for your mind, that TRICKSTER, to divert you into another direction, but you can be sure that your knowingness will always pull you back to YOU.

"Oh, 'he' is not bad, he simply asks you the same questions repeatedly: WHAT are you? WHO are you? Are you in THERE? Can you be YOURSELF? Are you yourself enough to STAND your ground? Can the rest of us TRUST you to, be YOU?... to be US? I guess, it is partly how the black dragon talks about unintegrated aspects, before they become facets of THAT.

"Take it or leave it, baby! Well, you can't leave it, so... you're the boss. Take on your big-girl pants, as Sar'h says, roll up the sleeves and show them what you ALL are made of!"

Laura is here, and she laughs. "Oh, you talk about Carl! Well, he is a she these days, so maybe Carla is more correct!"

EQ: "Laura, last time we spoke, you told me you are one of the 'good deed doers' in the life you have now."

"I sat down with you a few weeks ago, when you watched some of 'The Good Witch' movies from 2008 to 2011, I guess. Quite old stuff, even in your time. I was stunned to see me as Laura mirrored to such a degree by the character, Cassie Nightingale: An energy trinket and a few words to point people into a slightly different direction than the one they are currently steering, but still operating in their pool of opportunities."

Laura continues to talk about what she observes in her life. I can feel her love for humanity pretty strong. "People know what they want, but often take some strange paths to get there, because of limited visibility, in the form of lack of sensing. They often get distracted on that path too."

EQ: "I guess there are no witches in your time."

"Correct! Even if we don't give the term a proper definition."

"And you're not selling tobacco and alcohol."

"Correct again."

"But you are selling PRINTED books!"

"Yes, good old fashion printed books on paper which I have 3D-printed myself, and with ink of my own making... and the glue!"

"But you can't have a high demand and selling worldwide when you produce all the raw materials yourself?"

"But dear, it only takes a printer next to the customer to get them a physical copy."

"But it can't be on your paper using your ink."

"Yes, it can. You've heard of a concept call a recipe? The customer downloads ALL the necessary information to pull a book out of the air. See, THAT is cool! A book from nothing but code! Hint, hint!"

"And copyright?"

"The author holds the copyright to the story and the artist the copyright to the artwork. We have the official *prevention and data security system* for the data downloaded. Besides the copyright, there is a patent system, but it is highly restricted... taught us by bitter experience...

"Every material can be analysed and replicated, and anything can be scanned and turned into a 3D model and then produced in different ways if one really wants to. Everything is different in my time, law, economy, energy... well, life. You can't compare it to any degree, because the foundation for life and the values have changed drastically. You don't hold a higher status because of a well-paid job, but you will get attention is you have an INTERESTING job! Furthermore, my customers are not the cheating type."

EQ: "How about family?"

"I suppose you mean my family. Things have changed greatly regarding this too. Because of the longer lifespan, staying together as a family of kids, parents, grandparents and even more generations doesn't make much sense. We choose more individual lives with people we like rather than putting the family first. Help is given to those who need it, it's not up to the family. This is one of many emotional pressures that has been taken away from a person... to obtain the goal of 'the easy life'. Now people don't have the excuse to choose to suffer to get pitied to gain attention.

"I live in proximity to some of the masters of your time, even if distance is of no concern to us who meet in consciousness."

"Do you have pets?"

"I have a through and through and hundred percent old fashioned birthed cat. He was named August by the animal shelter from where I picked him up as a half year old kitten. With nine lives, August doesn't need augmentations, only a bit of bio-maintenance from time to time.

"We have different environments around here, and I can take him for walks in a dense forest, a rocky terrain and even on a sandy beach.

"I had to get a science permit to study animals in nature, especially at night, so we can take these walks. Thus, I'm also in some projects at the university."

"Where do you live on the planet, Laura?"

"I don't want to give you more hints for now. Approximately half a millennium divides us in environmental changes, so it doesn't really matter, anyway."

EQ: "You're in Africa!"

"Busted!"

EQ: "You change environment, beach, forest, mountain, by changing altitude."

"It's difficult to keep secrets from oneself, even centuries apart!"

EQ: "I guess it's because you're so cleaver!"

"That it is. There is nothing that a good-looking built can't do!"

EQ: "I understand that asking how things are with you... the answers will be mostly useless in any sense, but I have some questions about Mars."

Food on Mars

EQ: "Humanity is on Mars in your days. Can we talk a little about what's happening in my time about going to Mars?"

"Sure!"

EQ: "For now, the largest problem to solve for having a permanent settlement on Mars is actually how to be self-sufficient with food. There are many obstacles to growing plants on Mars that we take for granted here on Earth. Low temperature means heated greenhouses are a must and shielding because of cosmic radiation. Low gravity prevents water from flowing to the plants as it does on Earth, so watering is a problem, especially in soil, even when you have the water. The same goes for oxygen to the roots. Fertiliser must come from recycled waste of any kind dissolved in water. Can you comment on that, Laura?"

"Growing meat could actually be part of the solution, because it has a high energy density, so let us look into that first. Right now, your scientists have huge problems producing meat from cells. You and I have been into cell growing and printing in relation to the building of bodies and body parts for humans. I have also mentioned that it wouldn't work until you use bio-electric communication with the cells rather than bio-chemical. Right now, the most effective bio-chemical communicator comes from animal foetuses! They ask muscle cells to grow in a tank. Cells have a build-in self-destruction mechanism which steps into action when they find themselves in a foreign environment; hence, the stuff from the foetuses. Here is also no immune system, so production facilities must have lab grade, not just food grade. Very simplified, imagine instead, a tank with salt water and live cells. You can have any type of, for example cow cells, and via bio-electrical communication instruct them to build, not individual cells or a steak, but say a hind leg of a cow. When fully grown, you can cut nice steaks out of it or whatever. Grow body parts, not cells. Oh, and remember, insects are protein too. In the first years, you will need to add nourishment to the water, but later, you can pull this out of 'nowhere', as I have told you with electric energy. And again: everything is just code!

"Until you find out how to create stronger gravity locally on the surface, you could build large slow-running centrifuges to make artificial gravity, either on the planet or in low orbit. People can use these facilities for plant growth. I also suggest using the ground-based centrifuges as work and living places as much as possible, or you must spend a huge amount of time and effort on bodywork to keep you fit."

EQ: "The way you talked about gravity; I assume you don't want to hint on how to create a stronger gravity locally on the planet?"

"Your assumption is correct. Humanity doesn't understand gravity. To understand what gravity truly is will have huge implications on the understanding of physics and consciousness."

EQ: "It is in the same ball game as free and unlimited energy. This is something that must show up everywhere, so no one can claim it and use it for power, control and manipulation... hm, that is really the same."

"Nevertheless, you are right. Internet and open information are crucial here."

EQ: "How about growing plants on Mars, especially if we can avoid using artificial gravity?"

"You must dig greenhouses into the ground and/or cover them with soil for cosmic radiation protection. Then you need light to drive the plant growth. You could use radiation filters on windows to narrow the bandwidth of sunlight that reaches the plants, but using dirt as building material and controlled light and frequencies through lamps are cheaper and easier. Don't use soil as a growth medium. You can use a spongier material, but it is cheaper not to use any growth material at all. Divide each greenhouse in two, one part slanting one way and the second part slanting the other. This way, you can circulate water by pumping it from one part to the other when it reaches the lower end. The plants' roots will hang down into the water, which will contain nutrients. The nutrients may need to be added on each high end of the growth platforms. It will be obvious to add carbon dioxide to the air in the greenhouses and oxygen into the water. You must also monitor and control the air circulation. And most important of all, listen to what the plants tell you. This is a corporate work between you and the plants."

EQ: "I guess we can't grow fruit and vegetables in water tanks like with the meat?"

"That's right. A solution is to print fruit and some vegetables instead of growing them. You must obviously grow kelp, seaweed and algae in tanks with artificial light, as in the greenhouses."

EQ: "The benefit of printing food is that there is no need for more than Mars' gravitation. Besides fruits, root crops also need to be printed."

"You can grow root crops like potatoes without soil on Mars. Even in low gravity. The small potato plants will grow like the other plants, but they will need much more space below because it's here where the potatoes develop, from the roots. You'll need about two feet of space, and instead of water flowing here, you must use water vapour so the air must be one hundred percent saturated. All nutrients must be in this vapour, and it must be circulated with fans. The potatoes can be harvested by human or robot hand, one at a time."

EQ: "Well, THAT is cool!"

"When you get some decent robots up and running to do the farming and processing, you don't need people and so no food for them. A double gain!"

EQ: "What about grain?"

"Here, a low orbit revolving torus will work. No soil is needed and the robots will move on rails from the ceiling. The cross section of the torus ring may be a rectangle with rounded corners rather than a circle."

EQ: "Oh, and we mustn't forget fish!"

"I suggest you only transport live fish to Mars to have live cells for printing fish meat. I know it is possible to keep fish in tanks, but keeping conscious beings that way is not an optimum thing to do in my opinion."

EQ: "We could talk a little about C3 and C4 plants. C4 plants have a more effective photosynthesis than C3 plants."

"Well, on the paper it looks fine, but C4 plants require more energy for the process. In cooler environments, C3 plants are typically more photosynthetically efficient. I suggest you choose what plants you want rather than selecting C4 over C3."

How to start a colony on Mars

EQ: "What is the best way to start a colony on Mars?"

"You could either start early and do things on a trial-and-error basis with people, like you in a sense are doing now, or you could simply wait until you can send up suitable AI and autonomous robotics to do ALL preparations to set up a full functional colony, before sending people up. No matter what you choose, you could probably start up a normal colony life on the planet at the same time. No matter what, you'll need a weather and communication satellite network first.

"I suggest you let the AI and robots do all the work, including the trial and error. The first human colonies will be in orbit, because they will really not work on the surface at first, simply because people are sent there before the systems are actually functional even on Earth.

"The first colony for humans on the surface must be built at the equator because of it has the highest temperature, no matter if there is more ice at the poles. You must recycle all water you bring to the colony, anyway. The equatorial temperature is about 20 degrees Celsius in the summer. Facility building with soil covered buildings come first, but later underground caves are widely used. You'll have robots to carve them out."

EQ: "What about fuel production?"

"Solar panels on Mars on a big scale take too much maintenance. There is wear and tear from dust storms and they are constantly covered by dust which needs to be removed, preferable without scratching the panels further on. I suggest compact nuclear plants for energy production."

EQ: "Are those safe?"

"The ones you'll use will be safe, or you wouldn't take them to Mars, right?"

EQ: "Hm. When can we expect to begin the first colony?"

"You must distinguish between building a colony and using a colony as intended, because they are two very different things. There are windows for missions in 2033 and 2035 where you could send humans to build an orbital station, if you don't want to wait until you have autonomous robots to do it. From here, humans can control the building of the surface colony with whatever you have of AI and robots at that time. Use the time until then to get your grip on things rather than messing around in the sandbox with silly ideas. You must also know how to use body manipulations for Mars astronauts if they do not solve the low gravity problem before people colonise the surface. You need to make special low gravity bodies. They will not function well on Earth, so that is truly what you mean with 'permanent settlement'."

EQ: "Can you view historical records from my future, which is your past?"

"I can view historical records of my time, but I can't tell you that your future and my past are the same. They probably wouldn't be."

Terraforming Mars

EQ: "One thing is to have one or more colonies on the planet, but will we ever terraform Mars with conditions like on Earth?"

"No, that is unlikely, but we could, just not in the way most think of it, which is pretty naïve. You can do it with a conscious action like we have done several times on Earth. You redirect heavenly bodies like asteroids; that is how Atlantis was cleared out. Luckily, it takes conscious maturity to wield such things. The process could be as follows.

"Get the planet a magnetic field to keep everything close. Smash a huge and heavy object into Mars specifically, so it sinks to the maximum depth with a minimum fraction of the planet's overall structure. This will still be totally devastating to anything you might have placed there. The situation may take hundreds of thousands of years to settle without adjustments on your part.

"Next, bring a lot of water to Mars, just as it happened to Earth, by using a lot of ice comets.

"Move the planet's orbit closer to the Sun, preferable so Mars is always on the opposite side of the Sun than Earth. This will give a more stable environment on both planets.

"Add algae to the water on the planet and stir.

"Wait to ripe.

"It is a general recipe, but you get the point."

EQ: "It seems doable, but why doesn't humanity succeed in terraforming Mars?"

"Let us put the absolute biggest wide-lens on and take a look through it. We have Earth as a tool with a specific purpose: each one coming to the planet must understand consciousness and energy. There will be no support for the expansion to Mars, and it is not needed. A second Earth will course humanity to be very divided, which is in no one's interest. People can have their fun on Mars and in space in general, that is totally up to them, but no terraforming.

"A passing remark: This solar system has been placed on the outskirts of the galaxy by design. Furthermore, it is put off limit to extra-terrestrial civilisations, both physical and conscious visits for a hundred-year period, because of these sensitive times. Even the extra-terrestrial representation in the system has been ordered to leave... meaning physical death, if necessary."

EQ: "Does this mean that the channelling of civilisations like the Pleiadeans and Octorians is not working?"

"That is right. What may be channelled comes from the Collective Belief Pool which is not dumber than the average human. It sees itself as a god, anyway."

Back in France, visiting Anna

You know, winter in the British Isles isn't really my cup of tea, so I'll jump to the summer holidays in 2023. This way we also skip most birthdays, including Li's, seven years and mine, eight years. It is a double jump really, time AND space, because we will cover the Wang family's summer days on the French Riviera.

EQ: "I get the 'British Isles' and 'cup of tea' joke... kind of, Julia."

"You can read between the lines... or better, behind the lines. This 'reading more than what the lines say' is, of course, 'sensing the writer' if this was an ordinary writing scenario."

EQ: "And readers do this sensing all the time... wait, haven't we hinted at this before? I believe so."

Hinting is good! And you, reader, should always be aware of the connection we have... you and I, because we are the only ones here in this point of... conscious connection. Outside of time, we connect in this very moment... and now this moment... and now this! Quite cool, actually!

The summer in the UK is usually not cold, but leaving the relatively cold air on the plane, the warm air in Nice goes right into my being, giving me a warm welcome. I get a flash of a connection to a warm and dry Africa... Laura. You truly are never alone.

EQ: "I feel the warm and dry Africa, too."

Laura: "It's because I'm still here with you... as in always. There is no separation between us, except in the mind. You have sensed me for many years. I know that, because I've sensed you. Sometimes, when I felt I was going out of my mind and so out of my body, I stepped into your cold soothing air, which brought me back into my body. When you felt you needed to get outside in the night to feel the cold air, it was me who really needed it. So, thank you for that."

EQ: "It must be why this life has felt like there was something more to it all. You being just one of us connecting in. At the same time, I've felt, to some degree, shielded from strong influences from the physical world. Now I know, I have Claire to thank for that."

Claire: "It's always nice to have a dragon available, especially such a nice looking one like me."

EQ: "And I thought at some point, it was the masters and guides... but the only one who has been here the whole time is you... me... us!"

Julia: "Before the dragon steals the entire show, can we come back to France?"

EQ: "Yes, of course. France at the Mediterranean in summer in Nice. I'll just dry my eyes so I can see what I'm writing."

We stay at the hotel *Villa Dracoena*, so the shuttle bus picks us up with a few other people who will stay at the small hotel. Anna and the Nielsens are at the hotel greeting us.

We bring only some clothes, so Li and I have space for our roller skates and protection equipment. They will be the primary means of transportation we will use when we are out on our own.

Nielsen's has brought their car to take a few things we have brought with us, like presents, back to the house. Jo-Ann and Anna have brought their inline skates in the car, so Li gets his first crazy ride through the neighbourhood and Vieux Nice, Old Nice right away. Later we meet at the house for fruit, ice cream and cold drinks. Oh, and not to forget, that when we enter the house, the smell of newly baked bread tells us what to expect. To go with the bread, we have juicy and tasty sun ripped tomatoes with a little bit of salt.

Tomorrow they, meaning Anna and the Nielsens, have planned to take us on a tour in their sailboat to a suitable spot for snorkelling. "This will prepare you for other activities at sea at a later time," Jo-Ann says. This is where you don't peek into the possibilities for the days to come... you just sense the warmth radiating from the top of the stonewall on which I'm lying, while the setting sun paints orange the white ice cream I am enjoying.

The next day on the sailboat, while Li and Isabella are at the helm, Kurt talks about the disadvantage of the shore falling relatively steep into the sea. This prevents beaches with shallow water for thriving marine life, ideal for snorkelling adventures. Small islands outside the main coast would have been a haven for both humans and marine creatures.

I could have told him that in time, large floating islands with a likewise floating shallow seabed will dot most of the Mediterranean coastline. A raising population and a demand for leisure activities causes this, because people have more free hours. There are a lot of small hiding places underneath the floating islands to keep a high population of life around.

EQ: "But wouldn't the floating seabed take damage from the breaking sea during storms?"

"The floating shallow seabed can be lowered via steel wires to a calmer depth."

EQ: "How do we prevent the sand on the seabed from being washed off into the deeper sea?"

"Sand? Oh, sand is overrated. You'll have a slightly spongy surface at these places and thin rock or concrete surfaces on others. There will be a sandy beach above the water level on the island itself."

After having spent some time at an almost calm open sea, we return to shore and drop the anchor in front of *Plage Paloma*. Here, in the relatively shallow water, we have our snorkelling adventure. We see plenty of small fish and crawling things at the bottom, and are lucky enough to see an octopus when we venture a bit further out, and so deeper, into a less disturbed seabed. We are warned about stinging jellyfish, but we don't need those around, so we do not encounter any. When sailing back, we have a dolphin alongside the boat for some time. There is quite some boat traffic in these waters, so dolphins would not normally come close to the shore to avoid being hit by a speedboat's propeller!

We reach the harbour at dinnertime and Kurt decides to show us an alternative to *La Belle Étoile*, a restaurant close to it. This one is called *La Cantine De Tiflo*, Tiflo's Cantine. Both Thierry and Florian are excellent hosts. We spend quite some time on their large terrace, pointing to the southwest. This place is used by the locals, which is obvious because they only close on Sundays, and the opening hours are from 9 a.m. to 11 p.m. If you tasted the food, you will understand the reason for the locals to come here.

The swimming and a lot of fresh sea air on the boat has whetted our appetite. After the visit, content and with our bellies full, we use bus 15 to get back to the house. We stay for about an hour before the four of us head for the hotel.

Today, we are parachute gliding after a motor boat. It is called parasailing. There are three 'seats' on the parachute. Kurt is so much heavier than Li and I, so he occupies the middle seat when the three of us leap to the sky. The water is very clear, which gives the illusion that it is shallow, but when you swim downwards in the clear water, trying to reach the bottom, there is quite a long way to go before you get there. From up in the air, looking out at the ocean, the water turns a darker and darker blue colour and the seafloor disappears.

I arrange so Luzi and Ju-long have their parasailing without others peoples' company. They are so sweet together. Anna has her soaring trip with Jo-Ann and Isabella.

In the evening we dine at *La Belle Étoile*. We walk to the restaurant from the harbour where we berthed the sailboat.

After sunset and with the full use of our stomach capacity, we take bus number 15 back to the bus stop close to the house and, equally close to our hotel. Indeed, a great day. I bet everyone will almost literally fall asleep when they reach their bed.

Both the hotel and the Nielsen's place have a pool, but as we are close to the sea, most of the time we go there for a swim and to cool off. Next morning, I test the hotel's pool water temperature, but because of its chill temperature I decide my morning bath was enough. We meet for breakfast in the hotel's dining room. It is early. Li is quite excited about the day ahead, but I am sure we will crash from total overwhelm early in the evening. What happens is that Luzi and Ju-long take on a whole-day scuba diving tour and Kurt and Isabella have a day off from visitors. A small helicopter picks up, the rest of us, the tough four or just T4, at the official Nice harbour for a trip over the Nice area and into the mountains. Looking down, it is like using Google Earth, but with much more detail... and shaking... and noise. After the round trip, they dump us at a farm for an early lunch in a valley leading up to the mountains. The helicopter picks up other tour guests and leaves us. What awaits us is a horse-back riding trip to a small shelter further up in the mountains.

There are four generations on the farm, all friendly and used to visitors. They have mixed farming, crops and livestock, and supplement it with the tour guiding, horse renting, and a 'visiting a farm' activity. They have a lot of sheep.

A young man, Albert, from the third generation, will be our guide for the next twenty hours or so. After the meal, Albert introduces us to the horses. None of them are tall and slender, and I ask Albert what breed they are.

"They can all be said to be Boulonnais. No, it's not the sauce, which is spelled with an e in the end, so the s is pronounced, which is not the case with the breed's name. As you can see here, they come in many colours. They are good and strong work horses, and suitable for work in the fields, the mountains and in the forest."

To get horse and rider to know each other, we all spend time currying the horse. Anna and Jo-Ann know how to use a hoof pick and put on a saddle, bit and bridle, so they also prepare Li and my horse, while Albert keeps a sharp eye on everything and makes a last check. "We don't want any incidents in the mountains, where we are on our own."

Albert also instructs us in how to use the small radio, which each of us has in a small pouch in front of the saddle. "That is actually my idea. It is not practical for people to wear, because only a few would have a pocket it fits in, and to carry it around the neck is hugely unpleasant."

Li can't help himself. "Horse, now also with short-band radio!" Him and Anna are constantly competing in being the silliest one.

Li: "The funniest one, if I may!"

"Yes, you are both so ridiculously funny! But sure, sometime you hit gold... but only sometimes!"

The ride up to and through the mountains happens at a relaxed pace. Albert tells us much about the area, both bout the present and the past. He also knows a lot about how the landscape was formed and about its animals and vegetation.

Before we reach the mountains, we ride through a lovely forest where we made a halt at the most beautiful little lake. We stretch our legs and the horses bend their heads to enjoy the juicy grass and clover at the banks.

The moment explodes in my sensing, where the human senses are just a minute part. The light through the foliage, the shadows where the light doesn't quite reach, the many colours and nuances, the smells and the sounds. And not the least, the hidden life and awareness, which most humans can't pick up.

I make a decision. "Albert, I want to share something with you. Something you might not know about the place, of which you obviously know so much about. Come, stay next to me with the feet solid on the ground."

"Oh, well, yes." He comes over and spread his legs a bit to get a firm stand.

"I will show you the forest like I see it, but to do so, you must close your eyes, so you see it with mine. Can you imagine that can happen?"

"I guess so, as if you sent your sight to my brain?"

"Something like that, but also so much more. I will connect to all your senses, not only the sight. Close your eyes and sense your feet firm on the ground."

"OK."

"Now, without opening your physical eyes, imagine you slowly open your inner eyes like in a dream."

We hear a very long 'wow' from him, and I must grasp his belt to keep him balanced. He looks around, experiences this as if he was wearing virtual reality googles.

"Albert, don't try to explain what you are experiencing. Just be with it as much as you can stand it."

I give him some time to soak it all in. I know it will fade over time and become a memory in reduced resolution, if one can say that.

"I never want to open my eyes again!"

"This is what you sense, when your senses truly open to the world you live in. Well, the world in you. I tweaked your human senses to get the optimum experience, and I tickled your divine senses to wake them up a bit."

"What will happen when I open my eyes?"

"You'll still remember, but as you know, memories will fade."

"Can I take a photo?"

"Look at people's art, and you'll see some of them trying to show the rest of the world what they experience. You can make your own pictures too, right?"

"I feel vigorous and exhausted at the same time."

"I ask you to close your inner eyes and be in the shimmering light you see behind your eyelids for as long as you need, before you open your physical eyes."

After a moment, he opens his eyes and looks around. "So..."

"Don't say anything or compare it with anything. Just be here now and in silence."

With tears in his eyes, he bends down and gives me a hug. "Thanks Julia. I'll never totally forget this."

"You will not."

I sense his thoughts as he hugs me. 'She feels so fragile in my arms... just a light hug... but at the same time I know that there can't be anyone stronger than her.'

He lets go of me and I of him. "Everything talked to me, but not in words. Even the horses said hi!"

I smile, noticing the young boy in the grown man, seeing a true fairy world for the first time. "Everything talks to you if you show it that you are listening. Then the horses and the plants will tell you what they need, even the soil! The soil is not stupid, you know, but immensely wise!"

He wipes away his tears. "Few have seen me cry... and not for years."

"And some of us, some part of us, cries all the time."

We get into the saddles again, and I turn to Albert. "The horses actually said that from now on, you don't have an excuse for NOT meeting their requests."

"I'll do my best to listen."

"You must listen with you heart, with your know-ingness. Knowingness is not of the mind, so it wouldn't FEEL like the truth. There might not be a feeling at all, but you KNOW what to do. Then all it takes is to trust your knowingness."

We ride a bit before I have another comment for Albert. "Albert, just to be clear. A horse may say: 'I have a stone in my hoof, damn it!' No fluffy sweet talk here! But, at the same time, they are sweet and loving through and through... unless they aren't. They are as susceptible to life as any human, so they too have a past for better and for worse."

We leave the forest and choose a path that quickly narrows in, so we must ride one after another. Al-bert puts Jo-Ann in the front, then Li, himself, me, and Anna being the last one. Does Jo-Ann know where to go? No, but there is only one path to choose from and the horse knows. At some point, Albert directs her to turn right when another path shows itself. I see it leads to a group of trees in the distant. It turns out to be a valley with a small for-est and a few shelters. There is no cabin. A shelter is a low, raised platform with a slanting roof and closed on all sides but one. You can sit, but not stand upright in it. It is here where we will sleep tonight. The fire place on which we will prepare our dinner is a few metres away from the shelter.

There is a fence for the horses to realm freely, but there doesn't seem to be any water. That may be a good thing, because it cuts down on the number of mosquitoes that want to visit the place.

First, we take care of the horses, remove the saddles and bit, and Albert empties two fifteen litre water cans, carried by his horse, into the horses' water barrow.

Finally, we can sit down and enjoy fruit and bread, some of which we all share with our horses. Albert shares with us the plan for the rest of the day and tells us about this place. Later in the afternoon, we make a short hike to a small waterfall and lake where we have a wonderful, but cold, swim before we walk back to the shelter to cook our dinner. One horse comes along to carry the two, now filled, fifteen litre water cans. The cans are typical camping cans with a tap. They are made of soft plastics and can be folded when empty. Pretty cool.

Albert surprises us with the dinner. We all participate in preparing the raw materials, but if anyone will postulate that French cuisine can't be made over a bonfire, they are so wrong.

Before bed, we lead the horses to the lake by the waterfall. It is done in a nice, relaxing atmosphere, and the horses aren't wearing bridles.

"Yes, Eriqa. Here the word 'nice' fits!"

Back at the shelters, Albert pulls out mosquito head gears for all of us to ensure us a good night's sleep, at least concerning mosquito bites. This gives me an opportunity to show him a different side of nature. "Albert, when I sense a female mosquito in my bedroom or where I sleep, I communicate with the consciousness behind the insect. Some call it the mosquito deva, but it makes no difference. We make a deal that usually goes as follows. I allow a bite, which is really a sting, for the mosquito to get a full portion of blood from the upper side of one of my fingers. In return, no mosquito will disturb me during my sleep."

"So, you think it will work here?"

"We are invading the mosquitoes' world here, so to acknowledge their right to be here, we honour them by contacting their deva. I expect we can make a similar deal. Are all of you up to this? A mosquito bite on the upper side of a finger gives minimal discomfort, if any."

As I expect, all agree.

"Ok. I make the contact and am the spokesperson. Each of you can imagine facing a female mosquito as large as you, face to face. There is nothing to fear. The deva is consciousness, as you are, not a dumb blood sucker."

The consciousness of the mosquitoes has been with me all evening. All I must do is to make a connection between all of us. This happens outside of time, so the others, except for Li, experience an actual meeting. We are immediately back at the fireplace. I explain the meeting to the others. "You saw a large mosquito head in front of you, and you felt no fear at all. It was just sitting there, and you sensed a gratitude or love if you want to use that term. It was shared, because we honoured the presence of the insects and all what lies behind it. You may have seen the number 86, but that is your mind that somewhat plays with you. The eight is actually the infinity symbol, which means that the agreement stands until it may be changed. This is new to me. The agreement is usually a onetime deal. On this specific occasion, the number six symbolises gratitude for our acknowledgement of the mosquito's right to a place in this creation. This is so big too, and again, I am overwhelmed."

None of us uses our mosquito net that night, and in the morning we all share our experiences with the bites in the finger or fingers we felt or sensed shortly after we laid down to sleep.

Do I hear someone ask why we have mosquitoes? Because YOU, in your great wisdom, or naivety, created the opportunity of the niche of all these bloodsuckers, and so, you also created the reality for them to be in. Sorry dear, but the small suckers are all you! And so, all my suckers are all me. Can you love yourself so much you can acknowledge them, even love them?

During breakfast, I sense Albert is reluctant to leave the place. The latest hours have provided him with a great calmness, which he hasn't felt for many years. I know it is simply a reconnection to the land. Well, he has always been connected, but had forgotten to sense it. "Albert, we had such a great time here. Could you use the radio and find out if the helicopter could pick us up from the farm later? If so, they must notify our families."

"That's a great idea. I must ride to the junction where we left the path yesterday, for the radio to reach back to the farm. I'll do it right away."

He puts the bridle on his horse, but uses no saddle. Then he checks if his radio works and puts it in one of his thigh pockets now that there is no saddle and pocket. "I'll be back in no time."

Anna: "Ok, Albert. Meanwhile, we'll clean up the place."

"Great. If I'm not back when you're finished, you can bring the horses to the lake by the waterfall again and wait for me there. They surely won't run off."

Albert leaves us, and we quickly get the place to look like when we arrived. We, mostly Anna, even chop some firewood for the next visitors.

Jo-Ann: "Do you think it will work out with the helicopter, Julia?"

"Yes, the party they have planned to bring up to the farm is delayed, so it will work out like changing partners in a dance."

Li: "Where did that come from, Sis?"

"I have swinged my skirt in many lives here in France. Well, sometimes another person's skirt, usually wearing a moustache."

Anna puts down the axe, puffing after the unaccustomed work of chopping wood. "Let's leave the saddles and stuff and only take the horses to the waterfall. I assume we'll come back this way and it won't take much time to get the horses ready for our descent."

As soon as we open the fence and show the horses the way out, they choose the path towards the waterfall. They are used to this routine, and the lush vegetation around the small lake is a perfect and irresistible breakfast for them.

Not long after we arrive at the small lake, Albert calls us on the radio. "It is all arranged. They will pick you up at the farm at 17:00h. I'll be by you soon."

Jo-Ann responds: "Got it. We are at the lake. See you."

EQ: 17 is 5 p.m. 17 minus 12 equals 5.

The delay gives us an extra seven hours. After Albert arrives at the lake, we stay there for about an hour. The sound of the waterfall has a very relaxing effect on both, people and horses. Eventually, we fill our water bottles and walk back to the shelters to saddle the horses.

"Oh, I see someone has been busy with the axe!" Albert points at the firewood.

"Guilty as charged. I needed the morning exercise, you know." Anna poses like a bodybuilder with bended arms tightening her biceps. "You'll never know when a bear or two show up. One must be prepared."

Li responds to my inner 'comment' to him, because he and Anna used to have their ping-pong dialogue. "I have nothing to say, Sis. Really! I don't want to wake the bear killer in my aunt. Someone could be hurt... even me, if I can't outrun her. It is all about self-preservation."

So, we hear his comment, anyway!

Li continues with his voice: "When back in school, talking about where I went for the summer holidays, I can say with confidence that I had been visiting my killer aunt Anna, at the French Riviera." Then he whispers to me loud enough for Anna to hear it. "When we get back, we must check if she has an axe behind the door in her apartment."

"I heard you, Li. But you will thank me on your knees one day, when I have saved you from a fate worse than death." She makes some self-defence gestures and puts up a very serious face.

Albert breaks in. "Ok, check the saddle girths again and mount."

We begin our way back. It is already hot, and we all wear hats to protect our heads from overheating. We keep the same formation as yesterday: Jo-Ann, Li, Albert, me and last, Anna. Only fifteen minutes later, Anna stops us. "My saddle slides to the side."

Albert. "All off the horses and check the girths again. The horses have been eating and drinking, so this is to expect."

Jo-Ann helps Li checking his saddle and Albert helps me. It really takes some strength to tighten the strong leather straps.

Soon, we are on our way again. Sitting on the horse following its movements makes the body loosen up and find its centre. The horse and I have a strong connection and we share some of our life moments, mine, mostly being about my interaction with our pets, the birds and the cats. The fun things we have done together amuses the horse as I play the scenes for it. I can tell you; a horse can giggle on the inside and still look indifferent on the outside. The scenes the horse shows me are mostly very moving, but there are a few which show great fear or confusion. I make comments on all of them and the horse is able to get a better perspective of the incidents, especially the less pleasant ones.

We reach the trail that will take us down the mountain and turn left. Now our view reaches over much of the valley below, including the forest where we stopped yesterday. Albert asks us to step down, and he points out new places for us, and we take some pictures and make some video clips. Albert has some French syrup, cherry, which we mix with water. This way we get some sugar, and the taste is wonderful and natural. No artificial additives here. He also passes around some salty crackers, so our bodies can replenish the salt we lose by sweating. He asks us to share a cracker with our horse. They love it. Then we mount them again and are on our way.

Back on the horse, I sense into everything. For a while I switch completely to 3D and into the body. Here I sense the human body and mind, and this brings up memories from similar experiences of being in pure joy as a human. I had almost forgotten these sensations that truly makes the life as a human being worth all the trials and tribulations that come with it, too.

As we leave the mountain trail, Albert takes us on a different path back to the farm than the one we used on our way out. At some point I sense, he was about to ask me for another marvellous vision, but wisely he stopped himself, well knowing that having one experience to visit is much better than having to choose between two. The choosing will turn his mind... mental.

We reach the farm about an hour before we expect the helicopter to come and pick us up. There is time to curry the horses and say a proper goodbye. We hear the helicopter before we see it as a short black line coming up through the valley. We say our last goodbyes and the horses and Albert get ten stars out of five when Anna suggests a vote.

The helicopter takes another route back to the harbour than it took on the way out. Isabella is here to pick us up. This evening we dine at the Nielsens' house, and we have so much to tell and show. Julong and Luzi's diving trip doesn't get much screen time. It must wait until tomorrow.

Next morning at breakfast at Hotel Villa Dracoena Lu-long and Luzi talk a bit more about the dives, and in the evening, they will share photos and videos at the Nielsens'. It had been a two hours and twenty minutes' drive to the south-west to *Parc National de Port-Cros*, but they say it was worth it. Today is a day with nothing planned. It may be a day with too much ice cream, but Anna says that there is no such thing as 'too much ice creme', so I guess I just put on my big girl pants and dig in. I will spend part of the day reading, practicing my Spanish. I'm a good schoolgirl, you know. It is not dull work; I am in so many other places at the same. I also experience language as music. And Li? He says he will find a place, preferably close by, with horseback riding. Silly boy. He talked about a sore butt as we went to bed last night. He calls the Nielsens' to ask for advice and Isabella answers. Now the two of them will visit Isabella's preferred place. She hasn't been on horseback for a while, so it is a great opportunity to go there with Li. The dive-duo will cruise through Old Nice later this morning, and I may meet with them for lunch. Anna and Jo-Ann want to do NOTHING, as Anna emphasised, but they might show up in Old Nice to have lunch with us. Li, Isabella and Kurt will not be there. What about Kurt? Business, I guess.

I meet with Luzi and Ju-long in Old Nice. Soon after, Jo-Ann and Anna show up too. I guess it is easy to feel one's hunger in the state of doing NOTHING. They wear their in-liners and have some plans for after dinner. I wear my sneakers, because I want to spend some time with 'the old ones', cruising the narrow streets with one on each side of me. Somehow, that is what I 'need' right now. It is interesting to notice how the human part of me lives and develops next to me. I love this eight-year-old girl for what she is, in her complete trust in what we are. After lunch, when my parents and I leave the restaurant, we talk a little about human Julia and how she soon will grow into a young woman. She is the one who acts the human part of us, and so she is an absolutely indispensable part of all that we are.

Later, we have a lovely evening in the Nielsens' house. Ju-long and Luzi share their diving experience and Isabella and Li their riding tour in the vicinity of Nice. Kurt and Isabella, well Jo-Ann too, don't know the full story about the Wangs', but because of Jo-Ann being so special, her parents are open to that, Anna's family is too since the two young women are together. I know Li has made quite an impression on Isabella, and our visit this summer has loosened up things, also regarding Jo-Ann. Something that has never been uttered is Kurt and Isabella's wish for a boy when Jo-Ann was born. Li has gone deep with Isabella about none of us being boys or girls, and the fact that we have never been. And Kurt? You remember he was parasailing with Li and I. We didn't talk about the subject, but there came a crack in the shell, anyway. Of course, they will not change their daughter for anything, but old things tend to stay if not addressed directly or indirectly.

After a day of relaxation yesterday, except for Li's butt, we head for the harbour to attend water skiing in the late morning. It is a lovely day with calm waters and we are all here, Anna, the Wangs' and the Nielsens'. Some to attend and some to watch. It is the last day we spend in Nice, and the shuttle bus will take us to the airport before noon tomorrow.

Jo-Ann and Isabella are the watchers. They also work the cameras from the shore. The ones not water skiing for the moment are filming and taking pictures from within the speed boat. Kurt has a small diving camera which he can mount on his head, so we get some action clips as well, to add to a short footage of the event.

The water skiing is totally a challenge for Li and I. The roller skating has developed our balance skills, but a large part of water skiing is different. The instructor is competent and patient, and slowly we have practise enough to at least get a feel of how it is. Just wait until next summer! It goes better for Julong and especially Luzi, who has the experience of many holidays with Anna, Ya and Carl. Luzi and Kurt run a tandem show across the entire bay just to show off. Kurt is far the best of all of us.

We have a late lunch in Old Nice at *Alto Resto* which has an Italian-inspired menu card, as the name indicates. Alto meaning tall. Resto means both, a restaurant and taking a rest.

Again, out on the narrow street, Rue Fodéré, Luzi puts her hands on her stomach: "The French food has made me forget how much I love Italian food, too."

Isabella smiles: "If you are in for the ultimate Italian experience, and don't mind having two Italian dishes in one day, we can come back to the harbour this evening to visit *Les Amoureux*, meaning The Lovers. The place is a pizza restaurant that opens at 19:00."

Anna has obviously been there before: "Without feeling I totally betray French cuisine; we should definitively visit *Les Amoureux*! At least it has a French name."

From experience, we put our trust in Anna's taste buds, so it is settled. To get back, we could take bus number thirty-eight, but choose instead to walk the two kilometres along the seaside to Nielsen's house. Here we enjoy the rest of the afternoon in the garden in front of the house.

We return to Old Nice in the evening, again taking the coastal road to the harbour. You can't book at *Les Amoureux*, but if you arrive when they open, you are most likely to get a table right away. All seven of us get seated together on both sides of a long table. The room is narrow, but arranged well and it doesn't feel cramped with five to six metres to the ceiling, depending where you sit.

Indeed, the foods are delicious and the service is attentive. This makes people feel they are guests and not customers. The restaurant is only open for three hours five days a week, but the popularity makes it work well.

Out on the street again, I realise the restaurant has a large window to the left of the door, which can be open and used as an outlet for special occasions. Oh, there is another pizzeria next to the restaurant which is open most of the day and next to that one, a Lebanese restaurant! Luzi didn't learn from the dinner she had earlier today, or didn't care. I see her hands on her tummy as if she were pregnant. I do not comment, of course, and I do not begrudge her the joy of eating and feeling satisfied. A strong beer has turned her cheeks red and I am sure she will get a good night's sleep. I love her so. Tomorrow we will have brunch at the Nielsens' before the shuttle bus brings the Wangs to the airport.

In the morning we check out of the hotel, but leave our luggage there, and walk over to attend brunch at the Nielsens'. The shuttle bus with our luggage will pick us up there later, well in time to arrive at the airport before deadline. I do not feel sad about leaving. I can be here anytime, even though I cannot share my presence with the people here in the same way as when I am here in the physical. I *can* show up in the physical, but it makes little sense to me.

I enjoy the fresh fruit and mixed juice, newly baked bread and a hard cheese with a creamy taste together with white tea. Oh, and if I have given you the impression that the French eat a lot, it is generally not the case. It is very much about quality and taste, not to forget, time to enjoy the food and drink.

We say goodbye in the yard at the back of the house, where the shuttle bus picks us up. It has been an unforgettable summer holiday in many ways... and I can say that for all of us. Now we go back to the animals in the grand 'igloo', which have been looked after by Sarah, supported by her sister. Augusta wants to be our primary pet sitter, and, being very intuitive, she will. We get updates from the house's systems, if it has anything to report, but nothing has turned up while we have been away.

Gaia

Gaia is part of all of what I do. We are very close, and me and others are there to support her in her own transmutation to clear her from the 'job' of managing the planet. A job she has carried out far longer than any of us would expect. But as she expresses, "it is difficult to leave one's children, and I have shed tears every time a parent had done the same. I know humanity to the absolute core if anyone does."

Do not be mistaken. The human's lack of understanding of the wholeness does not burden her. The humans only burden themselves. In every given moment, there is NO WAY that the planet is not safe. I know you think 'nature', when I mention the planet, but the planet is so much more than that. I know you say that humanity can destroy itself and the planet, but plain and simple, we will never allow it, neither for planet nor for humanity. For your own good, tuck away that fear. It will only add to the situation. The phrase, 'don't worry, be happy' applies here... sort of. Focus on your life, and Gaia will focus on hers. It is not your responsibility to save the world, neither humanity nor the planet. The maximum impact on those issues is done when you focus on your own life. Clean up your own mess and act according to whom you really are, not what or who you think you are.

Sar'h gives a brilliant example of this as she is one of the beings joining Gaia: "Beyond duality, I ask if Gaia has any needs. She responds: 'It doesn't matter how much trash you pick up from the ocean. The ocean is the transmuter of all humanity's emotions, so there will still be trash there as long as your emotions are filled with YOUR trash. Keep allowing YOUR energy and consciousness to come together for YOURSELF and it will allow me to do the same in MY ascension."

I place a reminder here which refers to a previous chapter, but said differently: The mind can follow you out of 3D and understand everything if it lets go of the need to control. If it indeed is bold enough to let go and let YOU. As long as your mind doesn't fully allow YOU, it must stay outside of All. This is a big teaser for the mind, right? Be part of it ALL or NOT!

EQ: "So mind, get out of your cave and come along for the ride."

EQ: "One of the greatest examples of nature taking care of itself is how animals reclaim the Chernobyl area and thrive there. I have put a YouTube link at the end of the book.

"You might also find something about corals turning purple on the Internet, showing they use a different frequency of sunlight to the new algae species living inside them. These algae flourished in a time when the climate was much warmer, so it makes perfectly sense they show up now in a much more abundant way than it has in a long time."

In September 2023 I return to school attending Year 3, not that this indicates what I do at school. Li starts in Year 2. In our lives, we work 24/7, but it is not a workload for any of us. When the human part needs a break and calls for a timeout, it is no problem to grand it. We still work on other levels, as you might say. Li and I are very hooked on what we do, and find it highly interesting and what a person might call giving.

Julia's nine-year birthday in 2024

"I know it's a stretch to skip Christmas and New Year, Eriqa, but just think of last year's Christmas and New Year, and you'll get the picture."

EQ: "Can we write the age of each family member? I have lost the sense of that."

"Great, you lost it, because it makes no sense to keep track of people's age."

"But for the readers?"

"OK, for the readers AND Eriqa!"

Julia pretends to be impatience: "Well, I'm waiting!"

"Oh, I thought you have it all under control and could easily make a list."

"Control? Hey come on! Anyway, I'll tell you if my 'system' reacts to something in the list YOU make."

EQ: "To the best of my abilities, this is what has happened and will happen in 2024."

- Li will turn eight on August the 7th.
- Julia has turned nine today 6th of May.
- Ju-long turned thirty-five on the 6th of February.
- Luzi will turn thirty-five on December the 20th.
- Ya is or will turn sixty.
- Carl is in the beginning of his sixties.
- Anna turned twenty-nine on the 24th of March.
- Kong and Ting are younger than Carl and Ya.
- Ting is younger than Kong.

EQ: "That's the list."

"That's the list then. I have no further comments and we can move on."

EQ: "I'm waiting for what happens on your nine-year birthday."

"Well, the layer cake says HAPPY BIRTHDAY JU-LIA 9 YEARS."

EQ: "Do I have to drag it out of you?"

"OK, but I'll make it SHORT!"

We are celebrating my so-called nine years birthday, moving fast to be a teenager! It will happen before you know it. This time we are at the Community Centre in Hastings to take advantage of the bigger space and some of the other facilities. There are many guests here. I know so many of them, so I made a general invitation and posted it in the usual places.

On the day, I show a video we have remixed from the family video of my summer holidays on the

French Riviera in 2023... for those who have not seen it. Those at school have, of course.

We use the stage for the band... and me with a single performance... well, two, but only because I am forced to do so... and I enjoy it. We have three video cameras running on three computers covering everything that goes on at the stage. The instruments are free for anyone to use; and yes, some need a bit of assistance, but that is fine. Later on, the stage turns into an improvising kids' theatre play thing. The parents are in for a video editing course later this year, so the footage has a double purpose.

The weather is fine, but still, we have two large canvas overhangs to cover the foods and dining area. Some grills are running, and there is a bonfire further down the centre's garden. Kids love bonfires.

On my birthday invitation I have stated the Wang tradition: maximum one, non-expensive, but preferable personal present, and some food for the potluck. Luzi has organised the food part, so we didn't end up with like fifty similar dishes. I must say, you can find almost everything here, which includes exotic dishes brought by the non-British guests. They have labelled most dishes. There is quite a bit of Chinese foods, because Ya, Carl, Ting and Cheng are here too. The only one missing is Kong. He will be here next time, but he just doesn't know it yet. I drop into his sleeping state from time to time, and we always have a joyful time together. And the pets? Of course, they are here! They visit the centre often, usually by invitation, and I bet they know the place better than most of us.

Li's eight year's birthday

Now that we are at it, Li's birthday on the 7th of August, is not so different from the previous one. We give the party on Saturday the 10th at home together with Anna, Carl and Ya. A few of his close friends from school are here too, which includes the band. Li doesn't want a large arrangement like mine, but he has invited Augusta to attend, too. She has become a part of the family. In that respect, she has taken over her sister's place with our pets. More to it, she and Li are now the same age!

As a special activity, besides from preparing the food and the band entertaining, we have arranged a virtual reality multiplayer game. The game can have up to four participants at the time, each wearing wireless VR googles and hand manipulators. Those not taking part can watch the game in a third-person version on a monitor. It is a fantasy adventure game played on a local server, which is a computer set up on our local network. You can play it seated, standing or in a pre-defined space; we use a two-by-two metre area, now that we are outside. Each person has its own space so they do not accidentally hit each other, but they can of course meet up in the game. We need to play below a canvas cover to reduce the sunlight from interfering with the communication of the 3D positions between the components. I observe the game, this world which is very beautifully created can easily enchant you.

Luciano plays a role in the development, and also a role in the actual game. He invites me inside behind the scene, which I can 'translate' for you into a 3D experience, to turn into something similar to the Matrix movie series. In reality, it is consciousness and code, so it is NOT like Matrix when experienced from consciousness. It is SO much more.

September and school year 4

Another school year comes up, and it is business as usual, but the last one in this wonderful private school for gifted and special kids. Li and I will move on and end our physical appearances in the place, but we will still keep an eye on things and shine a light on possibilities if needed.

EQ: "Julia, this short text can't be the end of the book. It can at most be a short opening!?"

"But dear, there ARE no endings, as I said in the very beginning: there aren't any beginnings in my world either. Furthermore, if you had paid attention, I have jumped forward quite a bit for a good part of the story!"

EQ: "I have noticed, and I find it worked alright if one kept a focus, but I thought we would close with you tenth birthday."

"Hey, hey. In the story, at this very moment, with cheating and all, I'm now nine and a quarter of a year old. That must count for something. This is not the end, even I can see you have already written it a few lines down. Not an author nor ANYONE should TERMINATE a story... no stories ever end. That is just how it works. All stories move on, even if it must write the continuation itself! The story would never give up its life, NEVER!"

THE END
of this part one of the Julia Wang series...

With the deepest respect and compassion for your story, your life in all lives and in-between.

I hope you have enjoyed the book and ask you to take a moment to make a brief review or just a comment on your favourite retailer website or send it to me.

Hint: You may write it down now and share it later, or you may share a private note with me, then just state it as such.

Thanks in advance, Eriqa Queen.

eriqa.queen@erikistrup.dk

Author's comments

I have made notes here during the writing and after finishing the book, I edited them into a more flowing text.

Writing this book differs greatly from the last Luzi Cane book. It's as if still it maintains a connection to the entire story, but because it wasn't written through the mind, it confuses the mind more than it did when it sensed no connections. This time I was also much more dragged into the story.

It didn't take long to write roughly a quarter of the raw text for this book, but we were still in the first breath of the story, so I couldn't imagine how we would cover up to Julia being ten years old, starting the story before her birth.

This time, we wrote mostly the story from start to end. This was not the case with my previous five books. The obvious advantage of this is that you can always refer to what you have previously written.

We have already moved subjects that showed up in this first book to the manuscripts of future ones, because it fits with Julia's 'aging' and the general progress of the story.

Shortly after Julia had started school in Year 2 at age seven, the writing took a halt. Two days later, the rest of the story for book one and well into book two was 'downloaded' and the story was on track again.

Some places in the story may appear different from those in real life if visited. They are often selected by sensing into them, and so by 'energy' and not by appearance or function.

Oh, THAT was quite a ride at the end of this book, and I was totally unprepared for how we closed this first part of the series. It was much like going down in free fall on a roller coaster, which then suddenly stops right after reaching the bottom at the exit, while I still holding tight to the steel boom in front of me: "You can step out now!"

Life goes on, I guess, so here are a few comments on the cover because it may not be obvious what it shows. The background is the ocean, symbolising the Infinite Oceanic Self. This is also the Returned Self, the Third Circle, which is your home, you. The glass mosaic head of a woman symbolises all the human facets that integrate by the initial 'waking up' and from all lives. You are also seeing Laura, not Julia.

 - EQ

Additions

These additions are a continuation from the lists from the Luzi Cane series. Everything here is somehow related to this book.

Music

Amy Diamond, *"Higher Ground"*, 2000. Because being mentioned directly in the text, it is added here, though it's also in the Luzi Cane series. The entire song is about the human and the I Am relation.

Example of how expanded view can look with reference to Albert's experience at the forest lake: *"Viva La Vida"*, 2008, Coldplay, composers/ songwriters: Christopher A. J. Martin, Guy Rupert Berryman, Jonathan Mark Buckland, William Champion, **performed by David Garrett**: https://youtu.be/bZ_BoOlAXyk

"We are the World", 1985, written by Lionel Richie and Michael Jackson.

Films

"Encanto", 2021.

"Little Forest", 2018, Korea.

"Into the Wild", 2007, USA, 2 h 28 m.

"Ready Player One", 2018, USA, 2 h 20 m.

Books

"Leading the Workforce of the Future: Inspiring a Mindset of Passion, Innovation and Growth", 2020, Brigette Tasha Hyacinth. (I haven't read the book, so I can only vouch for the energy contents of it).

"Orbital Resonance", 1991, John Barnes.

Links

Links, especially to YouTube materials, may not work for various reasons. You may find the materials if you search the titles inside or outside of YouTube.

Adding smoke flavours to foods:
https://www.thekitchn.com/7-ingredients-that-add-smoky-flavor-without-a-flame-231019

Hemp: https://www.goodhemp.com/hemp-hub/
environmental-benefits-of-hemp-how-good-is-it/

Hemp: https://www.goodhemp.com/hemp-hub/
is-hemp-legal-in-the-uk/

Nodules: https://metals.co/nodules/

Wildlife takeover: How animals reclaimed Chernobyl: https://youtu.be/XaUNhqnpiOE